S0-APM-051

O'Rourke

O'Rourke

another slop sink chronicle

Kevin Bartelme

cool grove press

 Published in the United States by Cool Grove Press, an imprint of Cool Grove Publishing, Inc., New York.
512 Argyle Road, Brooklyn, NY 11218
http://WWW.COOLGROVE.COM

Publishers Cataloging-in-Publication

Bartelme, Kevin.
O'Rourke : another slop sink chronicle / Kevin Bartelme. -- 1st ed.
p. cm.
LCCN 2002141106
ISBN 1-887276-18-1

1. New York (N.Y.)--Fiction. 2. Humorous stories.
I. Title.

PS3602.A8384O76 2002 813'.6
QBI02-701492

acknowledgement
cover painting: Robert Bissel

First Edition
Printed in the United States

For Jack and Reid

TABLE OF CONTENTS

O'Rourke's Attitude 1

One fine April morning, had you happened to pass the corner of 104th Street and Broadway in the city of New York, you might have noticed two eccentric individuals loitering in front of the Thermopylae coffee shop before you continued on your way; a slack-jawed, middle-aged black man of modest stature and a modishly dressed, young white man holding a paper bag of the sort used to conceal beer cans over his mouth and nose. Had you stopped for a moment to observe these two, you would have heard the former bark out a few words of gibberish and seen him go through some spastic, dance-like motions while enough saliva to form a small puddle on the sidewalk dribbled from his gaping, toothless mouth. Had you caught his eye, he would stare fixedly back and given the impression that he was performing for you alone. You would certainly have noted the small bag that the young white man held to his face rapidly expand and deflate in time with his breathing as he moved back and forth in a tentative semicircle around the black man in some apparent attempt at communication. You would neither have known nor cared that the younger man was called Donald Little and the elder was known to the locals as Yo Bump.

On that very same fine April morning, master tile mason Robert O'Rourke and his assistant Maurice emerged from the 103rd Street subway exit and proceeded north on Broadway toward the condominium apartment on 105th Street where they had been engaged to ply their trade in two bathrooms and a kitchen. Among other things, Robert O'Rourke was a rotund Irish drunk with a penchant for novelty and possessed of a certain bitterness toward the mundane, stolidly humdrum world in which he was involuntarily forced to live. "It's all a mistake," he would grumble to Maurice. "I was born on the wrong planet but no one will tell me where the complaint department is located." Maurice assisted O'Rourke in his labors and acted in the capacity of straight man, audience, valet, apologist, confidant, and sometime stooge.

This particular fine morning, Robert O'Rourke was expansively hung over.

"I do not feel that I can function today without the aid of a zoid," he announced. "There are some zoids right over on that corner in front of the diner. We will study them a few moments and pick out the one appropriate to our needs."

They observed the curious interaction of Donald Little and Yo Bump for some time before O'Rourke made his decision.

"The gluehead. You are more political than I am. Go fetch him."

Maurice approached Donald Little with a congenial smile. "Hello, there," he said. "Brown bagging it today? If you have a moment, my associate would like to have a word with you."

He took Donald Little firmly by the arm and led him over to Robert O'Rourke.

"My good man," said O'Rourke, "are you available for a job of work? I thought so. We will pay you one dollar an hour and teach you a respectable trade."

Maurice was irritated by O'Rourke's magnanimity. "A dollar an hour?" he protested. "This zoid doesn't seem capable of even the simplest tasks such as sweeping up or going out for beer."

"I can see where you might think that, Maurice, but my instincts tell me that this zoid has great hidden potential. I will call him.... Agile Shoebill. That is actually the comical name of a racehorse but it fits this zoid somehow. Bring him along, Maurice. We are late already."

Reluctantly, Maurice took their new charge in tow and they proceeded to their destination.

The doorman at the building where Robert O'Rourke and Maurice were working recognized Donald Little and immediately attempted to eject him from the premises.

"Unhand that man!" said O'Rourke imperiously, "or I shall have you caned! He is in my employ and as such is entitled to a minimal amount of respect."

The doorman glowered and cursed in Spanish but he let them pass.

"A man does not know that he's a man until he is tested, Shoebill," said O'Rourke as they boarded the elevator. "I will tell you a story to illustrate my point. Many years ago, I lived in the country and took whatever sort of job came my way. Often I worked with my neighbor, Stanley Hodge. One day we were hired by a certain Mr. Hare to repair the plumbing under his aged and infirm mother's house trailer. The trailer had not been moved in many years and had settled considerably; there was barely enough room for a man to squeeze underneath, but Stanley, who was quite a bit thinner than I was, somehow managed to squirm his way to the drainpipe of Mrs. Hare's bathroom. I pushed him a monkey wrench with a broomstick and, after a great deal of effort, he managed to detach the pipe."

"Then we heard it, Shoebill, the ominous clunk, clunk, clunk of Mrs. Hare's walker. She was making her way to the front of the trailer towards the bathroom. We listened in horror as she clunk, clunk. clunked her way along the hall and finally stopped directly over Stanley"

"Sweet Jesus!" he yelled. "I'm stuck! I can't move!"

"Mrs. Hare!" I shouted, "there's a man working under the trailer!!"

"Don't do it, you old bitch!" Stanley screeched.

"Our entreaties were to no avail, however. The lady was stone deaf, you see. I heard the toilet flush and I heard Stanley yell. He took it, Shoebill . . . he took it on the chest... purple old lady piss."

Donald Little sucked his bag uncertainly.

"And that's when he knew he was a man, Shoebill. That's when he knew."

The elevator arrived at the seventeenth floor and the operator ushered them out with the surly disdain of a nightclub bouncer.

"So here we are," said O'Rourke, "the job site. It's enough to make any sturdy pillar of the community with a charming wife, six brats, and a second mortgage go out for the paper and just keep walking." He pointed to a carpenter who was assembling a bookcase. "You see that nailknocker over there? Two years ago, that young man was a common laborer. Now he's a cabinetmaker. He'll go on this way and he'll make enough money to get married and breed. That's what people do. Beats the hell out of me why."

The three of them passed through the apartment to a small bathroom off the kitchen.

"O miraculous alabaster vessels," said O'Rourke grandly, "whose clear water has arrived at this place through a mysterious labyrinth of ducts to make communion with sundry human excretions and from thence be borne back to the mother of us all, the uterine sea; o humble toilet, we pay thee homage; sink and tub, I sing in praise of your sublime elegance. May we, in our small way, do all of you honor. Amen... Mix me up some mud, Maurice, so that I may float off this wall before alienation and malaise render me unable to function. Watch closely, Shoebill. You may learn a thing or two."

Maurice mixed up a batch of brown coat in a plastic bucket and O'Rourke began trowelling it on the wall.

"You're not supposed to use this stuff under tile,

Shoebill, but I happen to know who's going to be using this bathroom. The maid is a certain Mrs. Gomez, a big, fat Colombian lady. She has fifteen children and every one of them is a narcoterrorist. One day she'll be sitting right here on the pooper after stuffing her face with rice and beans and bananas and whatever else Colombians eat. She'll cut a giant fart and that will be it for Mrs. Gomez. The entire shithouse will collapse. It will take a demolition crew two days to dig the woman out of the rubble. When the President commends me for my efforts, I will say: 'As a veteran, it was the least I could do. Narcoterrorism must be stopped at the source.' "

At that moment, a short young woman appeared at the door of the bathroom in the company of a large older woman.

"These are the tile gentlemen," said the young woman.

"Oooh!" the older woman gushed. "You did such a wonderful job in the other bathroom. Do you love the green line as much as I do?"

"Are you talking to me?" said Robert O'Rourke incredulously and looked away.

The woman was disconcerted by this odd response to her question. "I mean it's very original, don't you think?"

"Well, it certainly is if you find that sort of thing original," said O'Rourke without looking up. It was clear from his tone that this was his final statement on the subject. The two women backed away from the door like courtiers at the conclusion of an audience with the shogun.

"The client, Shoebill," said O'Rourke, "one of the more pathetic life forms on this teeming planet. She has no idea what she wants so she hires an architect to tell her. She is depressed by the results and endeavors to enlist even a common tradesperson like myself to ooh and aah in appreciation at her hideous bathroom. She, of course, has to live with it. Eventually the green line will drive her crazy. She will suddenly decide that she hates it. She will hire another architect to redesign the place and the whole sordid drama will repeat itself.

"We, on the other hand, have the good fortune to never set eyes on this dump again after we have completed our task except in the exceedingly unlikely event that we are invited to the housewarming. Personally, I would decline such an invitation but Maurice would probably show up, drink himself silly, and try to pick up some horny and available woman with a Lady Chatterley complex."

"A common affliction these days," Maurice

agreed solemnly.

"That other woman with the client is the aforementioned architect," O'Rourke continued. "Her doting parents invested great sums to put her through the university so that she might have a career. Now she does – sort of. She works for a large architectural firm and this is her first job. She is terrified of everybody – the client, the contractor, me, even you, Shoebill – and with good reason. She is, as you can clearly see, utterly without talent. She does, however, have a comely rear end."

Maurice snorted derisively.

"Maurice and I differ in our carnal preferences, Shoebill. He likes emaciated women who have somehow misplaced their asses. This is because he is young and ignorant. When he's been in the business as long as I have, he will come to appreciate the value of a 'wide load', as he calls it. Can I speak to you man to man, Shoebill? What exactly is your position on cunnilingus?"

Maurice laughed.

"Serious questions always make Maurice nervous and, believe you me, pussy eating is one of the paramount issues of the latter half of the century. The ladies are fully informed these days about the most obscure parts of their anatomies. A virtual glut of magazines and how-to books keeps them abreast of all the latest battles joined in the sexual arena with up-to-the-minute dispatches from the front on the status of vaginal versus clitoral orgasm, the exact location of the elusive G spot, the latest advances in marital aid technology, and the finer points of cocksucking. Armed with all this data, they have wakened to the fact there may be more to life than wham, bam, thank you, ma'am and marched forth demanding their due. We of the opposite gender, innocent of many of these late additions to the body of female knowledge, have been hard pressed to keep up with the ins and outs of the situation and, out of our loutish ignorance, have often failed to meet the issue head on. Many misunderstandings have, of course, resulted. Why just the other day – are you still with me, Shoebill? – only the other day I witnessed an incident in front of the very same Thermopylae coffee shop where we found you this morning. A man and his wife were engaged in a heated argument about money. The man had apparently spent the better part of his paycheck in a saloon the previous evening and arrived home in a disgraceful state. 'That's it!' said the wife. 'I've had it! You're a complete jerk! . . . and a lousy fuck too!'

"So you see, Shoebill, the argument wasn't really about money at all. It was about – how shall I phrase this? – *amour*. If, on the evening in question, the reprobate husband had simply taken the few minutes required to attend to his wife's needs, their disagreement concerning his conduct would have certainly been greatly diminished. Now, will you please fetch the medicaments from my bag, Maurice?"

"How about the zoid?" said Maurice.

"Shoebill is obviously high on life. He has not responded at all to my stag party chatter. What should I try next? Politics or religion?"

"Religion by all means," said Maurice, handing O'Rourke a tall can of King Cobra Stout Malt Liquor.

"Let us call it faith," said O'Rourke. "More mud, Maurice."

"Coming right up," said Maurice as he set to mixing up another batch of brown coat..

"Faith is a peculiar thing, Shoebill. It is the wellspring of hope, an impregnable fortress wherein one can dwell safe from the horrors of the world."

"Hear, hear," Maurice guffawed.

"I am not addressing myself to ye of little faith, Maurice, but to Shoebill," said O'Rourke. "Even in his present sorry state, I feel certain the religious impulse throbs in his breast."

"Hallelujah! Chalk one up to the jumping Jehosaphat."

O'Rourke ignored Maurice and continued. "Some years ago, I received a call, Shoebill. Perhaps it was *the* call, but I was too callow to appreciate it at the time. A woman asked me if I would be interested in tiling a monument. A monument, Shoebill! My heart leapt. Was I the one chosen to commemorate the Great Quality of Life Revolution? Did the Fallen Heroes of Fixed Income Securities wish to set themselves in mosaic on the esplanade of Battery Park City? The possibilities made me dizzy.

"I assured the woman, whose name was Alice Port, that I specialized in this sort of work and we arranged a meeting for the following morning.

"We met at her apartment in one of those anonymous new buildings on the upper East Side, where everything is safe, sterile and dead – but expensive. One must pay for those kinds of amenities. I rang her buzzer and the door was opened by an intense young man who looked like he hadn't slept in three days. It was he who conducted me to Alice Port.

"The woman was enthroned on a very modern piece of furniture that looked like the failed outcross of a dentist's chair and a dynel wig. From this unhappy conjoinment of fuzz and function, she pointed at me imperiously and ordered, 'Come sit beside me!' like Liz Taylor doing Cleopatra.

"Well, Shoebill, there was no place to sit beside her save the floor, and I was not about to plop myself at her feet. She must have noticed my discomfort. 'Toth!' she said to the intense young man, 'fetch Mr. O'Rourke a stool.' A stool, Shoebill.

" 'I am Alice Port,' she said while I waited for Toth to arrange my seating. She was one of these women who worry about their weight after the age of sixty and wear far too much eye make-up and are still in there swinging in the bottom of the ninth. She gestured at a framed photograph on the wall draped with black bunting. 'My husband was Ernst Port,' she said as if the name were a household word, 'the Grand Vizir of the People of the Light.' I scrutinized the man in the photograph. He had a pencil thin mustache and looked like a Shriner run amok in his fez and satin robe."

"This is beginning to sound like a Dashiell Hammett story," said Maurice. "Do you think Shoebill can follow the intricacies of a mystery?"

"There is only one mystery in this story, Maurice, and that is the greatest one of all – man's relation to God."

"Whew," said Maurice, "strap on the seatbelts." He turned to Donald Little and pointed at his paper bag. "You're probably going to need a refill for this one."

"Speaking of refills, I could use another one of these tall boys, Maurice," said O'Rourke. "Now where was I?"

"Waiting for a stool," said Maurice, handing O'Rourke a can of stout malt liquor.

"Without going into the arcana of the People of the Light's cosmogony," O'Rourke continued," let us say that the late Mr. Port was the founder and spiritual leader of a cult. Do you know what a cult is, Shoebill? It's a religion without sufficient endowment to buy off or threaten the newspaper publishers, politicians, and other such bigwigs who can either provide it with a veneer of respectability or consign its simple faith to the margins of the lunatic fringe. That the Grand Vizir of the People of the Light and his followers had been tarred and feathered by the media was by no means surprising. Some years before, Mr. Port had come to the attention of the authorities when his plan to launch a military invasion of Guam, install Don Ho as a puppet emperor, and build a string of gambling casinos for the Japanese was revealed by a disgruntled former acolyte. The press gleefully branded Ernest Port a traitor and a sleazeball greedhead. It was only the loony tenets of his faith that saved him from being taken seriously and perhaps even tried in a court of law. You see, it was Port's contention that Guam was the very navel of the universe. When the great apocalypse came, only those in the navel would escape God's terrible retribution for Man's sinful ways. There was a hitch, however. Those to be saved would have to be lifted into God's hands by means of a gigantic forklift. Such a machine would be very expensive. Why not let Japanese tourists pay for it?

"This was the gist of the story that Alice Port told me while I squatted on a tiny stool before her throne. Then she pointed at me and demanded, 'Are you interested?' I assured her the story was very intriguing –

'Forget the story,' she snapped and stared at me intently. 'I can see that you are the only man for the job. Are you interested in working on my monument to Ernst?' I asked her what she had in mind.

'Toth!' she ordered, 'show Mr. O'Rourke the plans.'

"Toth laid a blueprint before me. Mrs. Port explained, 'The monument itself will be of the finest white Carrara marble. Water shall fall from the top into a pool fronting on a white tile plaza.' It took me a moment, Shoebill, to realize I was looking at the plan for a two story tall urinal."

Maurice broke into laughter.

"I said, 'Madame, I would be honored to take part in such a project'. And I meant it, Shoebill. I had no idea what Alice Port's motives might be. Surely, her feelings toward her late husband must have been very complicated to commission such a memorial. I'm not sure she even knew what it was. But I did, Shoebill, and I saw it as the culmination of all my years on the bathroom floor. How many 'white tile plazas' had I set in miniature? Their number was countless."

"Amen to that," said Maurice. O'Rourke continued, "I realized that I had been preparing my whole life for this rendezvous with providence, that every tiny, hexagon I had ever installed had meaning, that there was a great master plan and I was part of it. The sore knees, the lower back pain, the boredom, all of this suffering had a purpose."

Maurice turned to Donald Little. "It taught him not to let the client walk on the floor until the check clears."

"Go ahead and scoff," said O'Rourke. "And mix me up some more mud. What I learned, Shoebill, was that there is a God. And what a fucking practical joker He is."

"A crisis of faith," said Maurice as he poured

cement into a bucket.

"I took Alice Port's blueprint home and figured out a price. It was not inexpensive. I sent her an estimate and heard no more for two weeks. During that time of waiting I began having strange dreams, a single recurring nightmare really. I found myself standing with Ernst Port on the plaza in front of his monument wearing a costume identical to his own, a fez and a satin robe. The sunlight reflecting off the white marble was blinding and there was the stench of urinal cake in the air. Port demanded that I lend him five dollars. I refused. He became very agitated and threatened to throw me in the pool. Still I refused to lend him the money. Suddenly, a great cascade of water roared down from the top of the monument with a tremendous flushing sound. I felt myself being sucked into the vortex that formed in the pool. I whirled round and around while Port roared with laughter and threw hexagonal tiles at me – tiles that I had set myself, Shoebill. I spun faster and faster as the water drained. I always woke up in a cold sweat just before I met my Waterloo in the sewer."

Maurice handed O'Rourke another bucket of mixed cement. "I thought only plumbers had that nightmare," he said.

"It would certainly account for some of their

peculiar behavior patterns," O'Rourke agreed, "not to mention that haunted look in their eyes."

"You don't still have that dream, do you?" asked Maurice.

"Oh no, I only had it during those two weeks that I was waiting for Alice Port's decision. It went away as soon as she accepted my bid. It was a fore-warning, though, a premonition that I did not heed."

"Jesus," said Maurice, "you've got Shoebill on the edge of his seat. What happened?"

"Mrs. Port called me back and asked me when I could get started. 'Right away,' I replied. By that time, I was champing at the bit. Where was the monument going to be situated? Mrs. Port was vague on the matter. She told me she had several sites under consideration and she would make a choice within the week. In the meantime, I was to consult with Toth on the details of the tile design. I delicately brought up the matter of a retainer. I told her I expected a standard payment in advance. She assured me that the money was no problem. She would have a check for me the next time we met. Or did I prefer cash? Did I prefer cash indeed! She suggested that Toth and I meet at my 'studio'. I suggested that Toth and I meet in a bar. Mrs. Port told me she frowned on drinking. I assured her that I was of the same mind and would see that Toth drank only ginger ale or near beer. My doctor, however, insisted that I drink a glass of tawny port daily – purely for medical reasons, you understand – and I preferred to take it in convivial surroundings. She was sympathetic but suggested I eschew alcohol in favor of 'brain breathing'. I told her I would look into that therapy.

"I met Toth at the Pig and Whistle saloon the next afternoon. He looked like he hadn't slept in two weeks and immediately ordered a Bombay gin martini straight up. He downed it in two gulps and ordered another. I started to discuss the plans for the monument but Toth didn't seem interested. 'Do you know this is the first time I've been out of that house in a month?' he whined. 'That old bitch doesn't leave me alone for a minute.' I was not surprised. Alice Port looked like a woman with a sexual appetite and I was tempted to ask for details, but Toth quickly disabused me of that randy notion. 'All day long she sits there crooning over this shrine to Ernst, making me chant with her for his return.' He leaned close and fixed me with a blowtorch stare. 'He is returning, you know'. Had I forgotten I was dealing with a crackpot religioso? I tried to turn the discussion to the task at hand but Toth was on a roll. 'Ernst will return in the body of another,' he told me. 'Before his death, he revealed that his incarnation would coincide with the next partial lunar eclipse.'

"What choice did I have but to humor the poor fellow? 'And just when might that be?' I asked. 'It has already happened,' Toth replied. 'More than two weeks ago. Ernst Port walks among us anew.'

"I asked Toth if he would like another martini and I didn't have to twist his arm. 'Very dry and very cold,' he instructed the bartender.

"I said, 'Let me ask you a question. If Ernst Port is back from the dead, why hasn't he looked up his wife? And why does she want to build this monument to his memory?'

" 'The monument was Ernst's own idea and design,' said Toth. 'He will appear in the mist from the fountain upon its completion.'

" 'You mean he's hiding out until then?' I asked. 'Of course not,' said Toth. 'He is here, but he doesn't realize who he is yet.'

"The commonest of problems, I thought to myself and decided not to pursue the subject further. I told Toth it was my understanding that we were meeting to discuss the design of the tile plaza in front of the monument. Hadn't we better get down to business? 'I am not here to discuss tile design,' said Toth. 'I am here to prepare you for what is to come.' He was now at least one sheet to the wind and beginning to slur his words. He ordered yet another martini. I'd had about enough of this nonsense. I told him I had a pressing appointment and got up to leave. 'We shall meet again!' said Toth.

"I behaved cordially and assured him I looked forward to it. Then I fled the bar. I heard the next day that Toth had drunk himself silly and required a physical escort out the door. I also heard from Alice Port who berated me for allowing the poor boy to wind up in such a disgraceful condition. She scolded, rather cryptically, that 'a man of your stature should be ashamed of himself'. As you can see, Shoebill, I am neither tall nor important. I wondered if she was making a digging allusion to my girth."

"A low blow, that," said Maurice.

"I, of course, defended myself. I hadn't forced young Toth to take the waters. I assumed that he dwelt safely within the tenets of his faith which surely must condemn that sort of overindulgence.

" 'Are you making fun of Portism?' Alice demanded. 'Because, if you are, you're in for one hell of a surprise.'

"I assumed she meant I would not be among those chosen for the forklift to the hereafter, but I had no intention of getting involved in another theological discussion. I assured her that I was not mocking the faith and moved right along to the plaza design. 'You shall once again meet with Toth,' she commanded, 'and not in a place where spirits are served.'

"I was willing on the condition that Toth show up with my first payment in hand. 'You are a suspicious man,' she said. 'You must trust me.'

"I said that I'd be happy to meet Toth at a place of her choosing which turned out to be the bandshell in Central Park because Alice thought that Toth needed some sun.

"Now, Shoebill, I'm not a man taken in easily by neurotics and other assorted fans of melodrama, but I wanted this job so badly that my reason was eclipsed – dare I say it? – by faith!

"I arrived at the bandshell at the appointed hour and found Toth sitting on a bench in the shade. He was not in good humor. In fact, he was seething with rage. The object of his anger was a group of conga players across the way. 'How dare those niggers make all that racket in a public place!' he complained bitterly. I suggested we move to another venue out of earshot of the drumming but Toth was not of the same mind. Before I could restrain him, he leaped up and bore down on the source of his irritation.

" 'Listen, you fucking boogies!' he shouted. 'Why

don't you go back to the jungle where you belong!'

"I immediately made tracks in the opposite direction and watched the ensuing events unfold from a safe distance. Toth attained his objective right away – the drummers stopped playing and stared at him in astonishment as he harangued them with racial insults. To emphasize his extreme displeasure, he kicked one of their drums. The response to this action was swift. One of the group grabbed Toth from behind while another went through his pockets and pulled out a large wad of cash. Then they picked Toth up, threw him in a trash can and departed with their drums."

Maurice broke into laughter.

"I got a pretty good chuckle myself," said O'Rourke, "but what did old Bertie Brecht say? 'He who laughs has not yet been told the terrible news.' The money that the worthy musicians had taken from Toth was, of course, my advance payment."

"Bad show," said Maurice.

"It was certainly inconvenient. But even more woeful tidings followed on the heels of this sad episode. When I next spoke to Alice Port on the phone, she implied that only a coward would desert 'one of his own' in times of peril. 'We Children of the Light know how to take care of each other,' she ominously told me. I replied that I was not a Child of the Light and that if Toth wanted to go around provoking people to kick his ass it was none of my business. My only concern was the construction of the monument plaza and we didn't seem to be making much progress in that direction, largely because of Toth's intemperate and unacceptable public behavior.

"Well, Alice didn't like that reply at all. She rebuked me for not understanding anything that was going on and warned me that I soon would. 'Before the week is out,' she said, 'all shall be revealed!' I told her I wasn't much interested in revelations at the moment; what I needed was that advance payment."

"You were still willing to work for these nuts?" said Maurice.

"I can't say I wasn't ambivalent," said O'Rourke, "and I really should have known better, but the monument itself had taken hold of me. I wanted to see it completed as badly as Alice Port did, if entirely for my own reasons."

O'Rourke was about to continue with his saga when Donald Little stood up abruptly and started to leave the room. "Restrain the zoid, Maurice," said O'Rourke. "We can't have him wandering around the apartment unattended."

Maurice put his hand on Little's shoulder and propelled him back to his original position. "I hope you know this borders on involuntary incarceration," he said to O'Rourke.

"Why do you want to leave, Shoebill? You are being paid to listen to me."

"Perhaps he needs another tube of glue," Maurice suggested.

"Put some tile adhesive in his bag and see if it hits the spot," said O'Rourke. "I have not brought you along this far, Shoebill, to have you walk out on me now."

"You need more mud," said Maurice.

"I need more beer."

"You shall have both," said Maurice as he handed O'Rourke another can of King Cobra and set to mixing up a batch of cement.

"My bucket runneth over. To your health, Shoebill, or whatever's left of it," O'Rourke toasted.

"Now, as I was saying, I felt that I had a vested interest in Ernst Port's monument. In fact, I didn't think of it as his monument at all. It was mine, Shoebill, it was the statement I'd wanted to make all my life, an epic rendering of the trickle-down or piss-on-you theory. That was the sole reason I agreed to meet with Mrs. Port again at the time and place of her choosing. She was not to bring Toth. She told me she would consult her schedule and get back to me.

"The next day, she called and asked me to meet her that same afternoon in the tea room of the Mayfair Hotel. I had never been in a tearoom, Shoebill, and had only the vaguest idea of the protocol. I correctly surmised that I would have to strap on a jacket and tie and get my shoes shined. I did the best I could to make myself presentable and arrived outside the Mayfair at the appointed hour where I was immediately confronted by a sartorial critic. The doorman treated me in much the same way as the doorman of this building treated you this morning, Shoebill. I hastily explained that I was meeting someone in the tearoom. He wasn't buying and demanded to know exactly who that might be. When I mentioned Alice Port's name, his whole demeanor changed. He started to laugh. 'Well, I guess that figures,' he said and ushered me into the lobby.

"Once inside, I could see why I was less than welcome. The tearoom was full of rich old bags and their piss elegant catamite retinues. They looked up at me as if I were a shit stain on the linen, but I held my head high and strode through that gauntlet of derisive contempt like Louis the Sixteenth on his way to the guillotine."

"Such a natural aristocrat you are," said Maurice. "I'm surprised the rabble didn't tear you limb from limb out of pure envy."

"As if that were not enough," O'Rourke continued, "Mrs. Port was waiting at her table wearing some sort of ridiculous headdress that would have only been appropriate on a Las Vegas showroom stage. She turned her steely gaze on all those old hags and their walkers and snapped, 'What are you all looking at?! I guess you've never seen a real man before!'

"I was by now in some region beyond discomfort. 'Would you like a scone?' Alice demanded as I sat down. I declined and opted for a bourbon and water. 'You will change your ways,' said Alice. I jokingly told her that she sounded like my ex-wife. Her eyes opened wide in wonder. 'So you know!' she gasped.

"At that point, the last thing I wanted to ask was, 'know what?' but what else could I do? 'Your body is merely a vehicle for the real you,' she told me urgently. 'Robert O'Rourke is no more! You are my husband returned to the living! You are Ernst Port!'

"Well, Shoebill, I guess I'd known it all along. Alice Port was a raving lunatic and there was never going to be any monument. 'Madame,' I said, 'I'm afraid there's been a terrible mistake. I am actually neither Robert O'Rourke nor Ernst Port. I am Napoleon.'

"That drove the poor woman right over the edge. 'You never were any good!' she screamed. 'You've never shown me an ounce of respect since the day we got married!'

"I egged her on. I couldn't help myself. 'I don't remember showing you any respect before or after that fateful day,' said I.

" 'The best years of my life!' she wailed. 'All wasted on a fool like you!' She was really frothing and she had the attention of the whole room by now. The maitre d' bore down on the table with frightful resolve. 'Excuse me, madam,' he said, 'but you are disturbing the other patrons.'

" 'Don't you tell me who I'm disturbing!' she snarled, 'you monkey-suited poof!'

" 'I can see this gentleman is upsetting you,' he said suavely. 'I shall have him escorted from the room.'

"So they threw me out, Shoebill. Not that I offered any resistance. I was more than glad to get out of there and offered the maitre d' a substantial tip to show my appreciation. He was not amused and scorned my money as he warned me to never darken the door of that tearoom again. I assured him that I was quite willing to comply with his request as I made my hasty exit. I was tempted to have the doorman hail me a cab but I decided not to push my luck and skittered off down the street looking over my shoulder to make sure that demented woman was not pursuing me.

"Years have gone by since that day, Shoebill, and I am still not altogether sure I did the right thing. Could getting dressed up in mufti and ordering Toth around and paying the required attentions to widow Port possibly be worse than what I'm doing now? I might be pursuing the simple life of a crazed beachcomber on some South Pacific island while I plotted the takeover of Guam if I'd played along with Alice. But no use speculating on the road not taken.

Maurice bowed his head. "Yes, we must live this thing called life as it comes," he said with mock piety.

"Go fuck yourself, Maurice," said O'Rourke, "and throw me another beer. I feel a great hunger arising within me, which means it's time for lunch. We will take Shoebill back to familiar surroundings and leave him to his own devices. He has been a fair to middling listener but we will stiff him for half his promised wage anyway. That, after all, is the American way."

"We're on firm ground there," said Maurice. "Just deduct the tile glue I put in his bag from his earnings."

"Brilliant, Maurice. Sometimes I think you missed your calling as a corporate bean counter."

O'Rourke stuffed a couple of dollar bills into Donald Little's shirt pocket. "Don't spend it all in one place," he admonished as he took Donald firmly by the arm and propelled him out through the job site to the elevator.

"Shall we take him back where we found him or just leave him to fend for himself?" said O'Rourke once they were out on the street.

"What do you think you are? His chaperone?" said Maurice.

"Quite right," said O'Rourke. "Parting is such sweet sorrow but this is the end of the line, Shoebill." He let go of Donald Little's arm and tapped him lightly on the chest. "Go forth and prosper, young man. You look like you've got what it takes to get over in this city and I expect you'll do well."

With those inspirational words, O'Rourke and Maurice left Donald on the street in front of the building where he stood inhaling his bag until the doorman came out and chased him away.

A Note from the Underground 2

Master tile mason Robert O'Rourke settled his considerable bulk on the stool adjoining young Maurice, his assistant, and hailed: "Landlord!"

The crumpled bartender turned away from the television set mounted at the end of the bar where several early morning denizens of the Pearl of Erin were attending the final countdown for the launching of the space shuttle Discovery and padded over to be of service.

"Can I get you something?" he offered in a voice that crackled like crushed cellophane.

"A double shot of Jim Beam for myself and a draft beer for this gentleman. He's not particular. Any swill will do."

"We serve no swill in this establishment but I'll see what I can do," the old man rasped.

"That's very obliging," said O'Rourke, "and you

shall be rewarded for your efforts in this life or the next.... or possibly the one after that."

The countdown stood at twenty seconds when the bartender set down the whiskey and beer in front of O'Rourke and Maurice.

"First time in three years," he croaked nodding at the television.

"A momentous occasion indeed," O'Rourke agreed. "The question – can America get it up? – will shortly be answered."

The bartender pondered this observation as he rejoined the hushed clutch of spectators at the end of the bar.

"Go get 'em, boys!!" an old veteran seated right down the bar from O'Rourke bellowed as the countdown reached five and fire exploded from beneath the space vessel. The old veteran's rheumy eyes gleamed with excitement and his red nose shone like a beacon as the Discovery lifted off and began its twisting ascent into the firmament. The crowd at the far end of the bar cheered as one and toasted the brave astronauts. O'Rourke looked decidedly sour.

"Listen to them, Maurice," he said. "They remind me of condemned men looking out their prison cell windows and cheering on the carpenter who is building the gallows to hang their ass! I prayed last night the damn thing would blow up right there on the pad and take out half the state of Florida with it but Allah has not heeded."

"What's that you say, buddy?" The old veteran leaned toward O'Rourke and bristled.

O'Rourke turned. "I said Allah has not heeded."

"I heard what you said, you sonuvabitch!" the old veteran snarled and shook his fist. "I'm a veteran! If I was ten years younger!

"But you're not," growled Robert O'Rourke, "so you can only sit there and scratch and jabber like your simian relations."

Maurice noted that this exchange was drawing attention from the far end of the bar and placed a hand on O'Rourke's shoulder. "Time to leave," he advised.

"Perhaps you're right," said O'Rourke.

"You know what he said!!" the old veteran bellowed. "Do you know what this bastard said?!"

Maurice and O'Rourke hurried out the door leaving the rising ugly clamor behind for the din of the traffic outside on Eighth Avenue.

"Are you trying to get us killed?!" Maurice sputtered. "You can't put down that kind of shit in front of the nuds!"

"You're right, Maurice. It must have been the whiskey talking."

Maurice looked back over his shoulder nervously as they turned the corner onto 39th Street and was relieved to see that no angry mob was pursuing them.

"Now what have we here?" said O'Rourke as a disheveled, scabrous bum who reeked simultaneously of formaldehyde and rotting garbage lurched into their path and urgently proffered a wrinkled sheet of paper.

"A canvasser for the Kit Kat Club, no doubt," said O'Rourke and took the offering. The bum weaved off into the street where a truck screeched to stop in time to avoid flattening him. This narrow brush with mortality seemed to greatly agitate the bum. He stood in place waving his arms and squawking unintelligibly as the truck driver pulled on his air horn. At the conclusion of his address, the bum reeled to the opposite sidewalk and continued on his way.

"A man with a mission," said O'Rourke respectfully. "Now read me what this says, Maurice. I don't have my glasses."

Maurice adjusted to the crabbed scrawl of the message and this is what he read:

HEY YOU MEN

YOU LIKE TO FUCK A LADY WHO HAD NICE FAT ASK HOE

NICE FAT COOLER. THERE A LADY I NO LONG TIME. YOU WILL LOVE FUCK HER TODAY. SHE WILL NOT RAT ON YOU OR WILL NOT TELL NO ONE SHE WAS FUCK. SHE WITH A MAN HE LIKE DICK TO. HE DRESS NICE SUIT SMOKE ALL THE TIME. HIS NAME IS TOMMY. SHE WEAR GLASSES BLACK DRESS WHITE SHOE NO SOCKING. WHEN YOU SEE THEM WALK UP SAY HELLO TOMMY CAN I SITE NEAR YOU. HE WILL MOVE OVER SOME. GO SITE CLOSE BY HER. PUT YOUR ARM AROWN HER. I NO HER GET HER GOOD HOT. TELL RUB YOUR DICK. TOMMY WILL WALK BUT YOU SAY TOMMY YOU COME TO. YOU TAKE IN OLD BUILDING WHERE YOU COULD FUCK THEM. WALK SLOW KISS LOVE FUCK COOLER PUSSY BABY HOE. ALL YOU WANT. FUCK TOMMY IN HIS HOE FUCK KISS LOVE 1 HOUR OR 2 HOUR. GOOD LUCK. YOU WILL LOVE IT RIGHT HERE. GO MAN GET YOUR DICK HOT.

— OK BROTHER

Maurice looked up.

"Astonishing," said O'Rourke. "I find myself very much moved. Perhaps if we hang about we can get a glimpse of this courtship procedure. We shall purchase beer in the bodega over here and stake out the block."

"You don't actually believe...." Maurice protested.

"I have an instinct about this one, Maurice. It must be the same feeling a big game hunter gets just before the lion emerges from the tall grass."

At that very moment, as if O'Rourke had conjured them, a well dressed man and an expensive looking woman appeared across the street. The woman's blonde hair was pulled back in a chignon with a big black bow. She wore dark glasses and a black dress. The man was tall and urbane in a blue blazer and ascot. His hair was slicked back, he was eggplant tanned and he smoked a cigarette.

"Look!" O'Rourke pointed out excitedly. "Could it be?"

The man and woman stood together but did not speak to each other as they looked up and down the street anxiously. Soon a gentleman they seemed to know approached. The new arrival's furtive manner, seedy clothing and ghastly pallor suggested a life misspent on the shady side of the street. Nevertheless, the elegantly dressed couple was obviously delighted to see him and, after exchanging a few words, they all three adjourned down a garbage-strewn alley and disappeared into a loading bay.

O'Rourke was awe-stricken. "Do my eyes deceive me, Maurice? I can only imagine what indecencies are being committed in that loading bay at this very moment."

"I'll bet you can," said Maurice.

"Go fetch us some refreshment." O'Rourke handed Maurice two crumpled bills. "I will remain here on watch."

When Maurice returned with two cans of beer,

each in its own tiny paper bag, the woman and the two men had not reappeared in the alley.

"They are certainly taking their time," said O'Rourke. "We can only hope that our informant was exaggerating his stamina."

Maurice looked at his watch. "We're supposed to be on Barrow Street in forty-five minutes."

"You know, Maurice, I saw something like this many years ago when I was in the navy. I was stationed on Treasure Island in San Francisco Bay where I worked as a weatherman. Every so often the fleet would put in and the sailors would be housed in barracks while their ships were fumigated. Now, you know, Maurice, there are a lot of terrible jobs in the navy, a deck ape on an aircraft carrier, for example, or a shell loader on a battleship. The worst job by far, though, is machinist's mate, the poor devils down in the engine room. These engines are so huge that they have no casing and the giant pistons must be constantly hosed down with torrents of oil. The clangor is deafening; the heat is excruciating. It is, in short, a hell on earth."

"Water," Maurice corrected.

"Quite right," said O'Rourke. "Now, when a ship put into port, these machinist's mates were rounded up and forced to leave their dark nether world for the light of day. I would watch them as they emerged from the hatchways and blinked in the sun. They were as white as grubs that live under a rock. Their long, stringy hair – quite startling on a man at that time – shimmered with grease. No amount of soap could wash out all that engine oil."

"What do you mean 'forced'?" Maurice interrupted. "Weren't they happy to get out of there?"

"They were not," said O'Rourke. "The engine room had taken over their souls. Their dedication to their infernal machines bordered on worship. Given the choice, they would never have left the oily mist of that cavern far beneath the deck. They looked upon the world of sunlight and fresh air with sullen hostility as they came down the gangplank and faced all the curious eyes gawking at them as if they were creatures from another planet.

"One of these gawkers was a certain Miss Quint, the maiden daughter of the base commander. Miss Quint was in her mid-thirties and no looker but she had an attractive air of desperation about her. No doubt, there were plenty of men on the base who would have obliged Miss Quint, but she only had eyes for these oleose machinist's mates. Nostalgie de boue, I believe the French call it.

"On some pretext or other, she lured three or four of them into her car and took off for San Francisco where she had a special arrangement with a motel owner on Lombard Street. What happened in that room I can only conjecture, but when Miss Quint returned her bedraggled charges to their ship the following day, she fairly glowed. As they lurched and staggered up the gangplank, she stood on the dock for all to see, waving and blowing kisses. Nine months later she dropped a litter of grease monkeys. Little devils they were too."

"What did her father think about that?" said Maurice.

"Commander Quint? The man never had a thought in his life."

"Here they come," Maurice observed. O'Rourke looked over his shoulder as the unlikely trio emerged from the shadows of the alley.

"The time has come, Maurice. We must complete our investigation."

"What do you mean?" said Maurice dubiously. The couple parted company with their furtive companion and walked off in the direction of Seventh Avenue.

"We must act quickly!" said O'Rourke. "Follow me!"

"Leave me out of this." Maurice threw up his hands and backed away.

"Your lack of curiosity amazes me," said

O'Rourke and hurried off up the street after the couple. Maurice reluctantly followed at a circumspect distance.

O'Rourke quickly overtook his quarry. "Alright, Tommy," he said softly, "I think we better have a little talk."

To O'Rourke's delighted surprise, this brazen gambit caused the elegantly dressed man to stop dead in his tracks. His tan faded as the blood drained from his face. The woman looked on curiously, chewing gum with her mouth open.

"Wh – who are you?" "Tommy" stammered.

"I want to be your friend, Tommy," said O'Rourke. "I want to be her friend too."

"I – I don't understand."

"I think you do, Tommy."

"You're not the police, are you?" said the man.

"Oh no," said O'Rourke.

"We – we don't want any trouble," the man stammered. He reached into his pocket and pulled out several tiny glass vials and shoved them at O'Rourke. Each contained a small white crystal. "That's all of it. I swear."

O'Rourke looked at the vials, then back up at "Tommy". "What do you take me for?" he demanded indignantly. "Do you really think you can put me off so easily? Back in your pocket with those things!"

"Who are you guys anyway?" said the woman. She had not failed to notice Maurice standing nearby. O'Rourke was surprised by her frank Long Island accent. "You look like artists to me."

"Artists!" O'Rourke blustered. "I've been called a lot of things in my life but that is the lowest! We are the very antithesis of artists! Artists create surfaces to illuminate; we create surfaces to be wiped clean. The artist seeks out uncomfortable truths; we cover up and sanitize the grim underlay of the world. Cosmetology is our business."

"You do make-up?" said the baffled woman.

"Yes, that's it precisely. An important job it is too. That silly spaceship orbiting the earth at this very moment could not return without a layer of ceramic pancake to cushion its re-entry."

"Tommy" was looking more and more bent out of shape. "I don't understand any of this," he complained.

"And you never will, from the looks of you," said O'Rourke.

"We do tile," Maurice explained. "The space shuttle is covered with tile."

"That's right," said O'Rourke, "but enough

about us." He turned to the woman. "We have it on excellent authority that you put out. Him too. My informant assured me that you'd be nice to us."

"Put out?! For a creepy old fart like you?" the woman guffawed. "You must be crazy!"

"Creepy old fart?"

"What are we doing talking to these nuts?" said the woman. "Let's get out of here."

She took the well-dressed man by the arm and pulled him along.

"Is it a matter of money?!" O'Rourke shouted after them as they hurried off down the street. "I'm very reasonable! What are you laughing at, Maurice?"

"You must have missed something in the instructions."

"I admit I didn't follow them to the letter but, at my age, I have neither the time nor the inclination to engage in protracted foreplay. Do you suppose I should have played coy?"

"You could at least have taken the drugs."

"And done what with them?" O'Rourke retorted. "Have you become an aficionado of crack? No, it is far better that we walk away from this encounter unsullied by the sordid traffic in narcotics. Just say no! I say."

"Sour grapes."

These were the last words Maurice uttered before he was grabbed from behind and pinned against the building wall by a beefy, young man in a blue windbreaker and jeans. At the same time, O'Rourke was pushed up against a parked car by two more undercover cops. One of them, a tall black man, quickly patted him down and went through his pockets.

"Where is it!" he barked.

"Where is what?!" said O'Rourke.

"Don't get smart with me, fatso!"

"Not only do you visit violence on my person," O'Rourke complained, "but you publicly humiliate me by calling attention to my unfortunate glandular condition."

"Your glandular condition is going to get plenty more unfortunate if you don't give it up," the cop snarled. "Maybe your friend's the one who's holding."

"He's clean," said the cop who had Maurice pinned against the building.

"I'm sure this is all a misunderstanding," said O'Rourke. "I myself am a lapsed member of the Ancient Order of Hibernians and my associate is a Young Republican. We have nothing but the greatest respect for the law and the brave boys in blue who enforce it."

The black cop tapped O'Rourke on the chest. "Now you listen to me, you mick bastard, and you listen good. If I ever see you or your friend on this block again, I'm going to shove a sack of potatoes right up your ass. You hear me?"

"Yes, of course, officer. We were just leaving anyway. Are you coming, Maurice?"

O'Rourke and Maurice hurried away toward Seventh Avenue, leaving the three plainclothesmen staring after them.

"Did I ever tell you the story of the two nights I spent in the Bergen County Jail, Maurice?" asked O'Rourke as they rounded the corner.

"No you didn't," said Maurice, "and I'm not in the mood to hear it right now."

"Yes, I can understand that. I hope you don't blame me for that little imbroglio. If I'd taken your advice and kept the drugs, we'd be on our way to the hoosegow."

"If you'd taken my original advice we wouldn't have gotten involved in the first place," Maurice countered.

"Where is your curiosity?" said O'Rourke. "Don't answer that. Let us not recriminate. We are still free to walk the streets and get in even more trouble. Can I buy you a beer?"

With that, O'Rourke and Maurice adjourned to the nearest watering hole, a small bar frequented by Puerto Rican crack pushers, and quite forgot their appointment on Barrow Street.

O'Rourke Gets it Wholesale 3

The accumulated snow on the evergreens lining the highway weighed on their branches so heavily that they looked as if they were in pain. The road had been hastily plowed and salted after the storm but it was still slick enough to blame for the tractor-trailer laying on its side across the two northbound lanes, causing the traffic jam in which master tile mason Robert O'Rourke and his assistant Maurice found themselves immobilized.

"What are we doing here?" Maurice moaned. "We must be insane."

"We are only greedy," said O'Rourke, "a garden variety form of lunacy."

A state trooper car sped by their rent-a-truck on the shoulder of the road with its siren screaming.

"Fucking cops," Maurice complained.

"They are only trying to make their presence generally known to dissuade these frustrated people around us from getting out of their cars and blasting away at their good neighbors with whatever artillery they have at hand. Have you noticed the extraordinary number of gun racks around here?"

O'Rourke and Maurice were on their way to somewhere they'd never been before, the village of Glandville, east of the Springs. Glandville was the milling center for the slate quarries that surrounded it and O'Rourke's purpose was to purchase a ton and a half of green slate tiles at a greatly reduced price from what he would have to pay in the city. It had not been an auspicious inaugural journey.

They had blown a tire in Stoatsburg and very nearly run out of gas near Saudades before they realized that the gauge on the dashboard wasn't functioning. In Albany, they had been held up by road construction and forced to take an elaborate detour to the Northway where they now sat a little way past the Roboville exit, fuming about their bad luck.

"They'll need a bulldozer to clear that thing off the road," Maurice grumbled.

"Perhaps we should take the fabled waters of the spa when we arrive in the Springs," O'Rourke suggested. "They will soothe your frazzled nerves."

"If we arrive in the Springs," said Maurice sourly.

"The impatience of youth," said O'Rourke.

"Surely you don't think we will be stuck on this highway forever." He had no sooner spoken than the biggest tow truck they had ever seen rumbled down a southbound lane in the wrong direction, heading for the wreck.

"You see," said O'Rourke, "help is on the way."

"I've got to check this out," said Maurice.

"So we shall," said O'Rourke. "It isn't everyday you get to watch the authorities try to deal with such a large piece of industrial detritus."

They stepped down from the cab onto the salted road and met the shock of the frigid air head-on.

"Jesus, that's enough to freeze your dick off," Maurice muttered with billowing breath as they crunched up the highway between stalled cars to the scene of the accident. The trailer, which was badly smashed, had been detached from the overturned tractor and the giant tow truck was attempting to push it off to the side of the road with a bumper assembled from heavy-duty black pipe.

"My God," said O'Rourke, "it's like an old Japanese horror movie – Godzilla and Smog Monster locked in mortal combat before the helpless masses." He frowned. "Suddenly I feel a sense of foreboding. This wreckage may be an omen. Perhaps we should turn back and forget the whole thing."

"You could have talked me into it fifteen minutes ago," said Maurice, "but not now. There's got to be some kind of pay-off after all this suffering."

"When was it you adopted this atavistic, religioso attitude?" said O'Rourke. "Do you actually believe there's some kind of justice in this world?"

"No," said Maurice, "I only believe that things can't get any worse."

"We shall see," said O'Rourke as they walked back to their truck. "Surely you know the story of the Springs Dairy Queen counterman who was working when Death walked in and ordered a vanilla cone. The counterman panicked, ran out of the store and drove off to hide out with his cousin in Glandville. When Death, who had absent-mindedly left his Racing Form at the Dairy Queen, came back to reclaim it, the manager asked him what he had said to the counterman to make him behave in such a manner. Death replied that the poor lad was just surprised to see him in the Springs because they had an appointment in Glandville for that very evening. So you see, Maurice, there's a moral here somewhere."

"And just what might that be?"

"No idea. I was hoping you could tell me." They got back in the truck and were able to resume their journey shortly thereafter. They did not stop in the Springs, which lay slightly to the west, but turned off the Northway and headed east on a two lane highway that curved along the course of the frozen

Spuytenkill into rolling farm country punctuated with stands of snow-covered pine.

"Pretty bleak out here," Maurice observed. "I wonder what the locals do all winter."

"It is better not to know," said O'Rourke. "As two of the century's preeminent homespun philosophers, Franklin Delano Roosevelt and Charles Manson, said respectively: 'We have nothing to fear but fear itself' and 'Paranoia is total awareness.' Syllogistically, one arrives at the formula, 'We have nothing to fear but total awareness, an axiom not taken lightly by our rulers and betters who do everything possible to keep us in a state of abject ignorance, which, as we know, is bliss."

"Ask a stupid question..." Maurice muttered.

"What is this I see before me?" said O'Rourke and pointed ahead off to the right of the road. There stood an immense, one story, windowless, concrete structure surrounded by a spacious parking lot that was nearly vacant except for a few cars clustered near the doorway. A peeling sign on the side of the building spelled out in script: HAPPY SHOPPER DISTRESSED CANNED GOODS OUTLET.

"Shopping has rarely made me happy," said O'Rourke, "but we can, perhaps, put a distressed six-pack of beer out of its misery."

They turned into the lot and followed the slushy track the other cars had made in the snow up close to the entrance. There they parked and went into the store.

The cavernous interior was brightly lit by bare fluorescent bulbs and laid out like any other supermarket with long aisles of canned goods and several checkout counters. A young girl in a light blue uniform stood behind one of these counters idly paging through a sensational tabloid with the headline: GRACE KELLY APPEARS AT LOURDES. A Muzak version of "Me and Bobby McGee" wafted through the overheated air. There were no happy shoppers to be seen.

Immediately off to O'Rourke and Maurice's left was a double glass door labeled AL'S DISCOUNT LIQUOR which appeared to be a separate enterprise from the Happy Shopper.

"We shall first pay a visit on Al," said O'Rourke. "If all goes well, we may be able to avoid getting involved in the rest of this forbidding place."

They passed through the double glass door and entered into a large round room, the walls of which were covered with racks of liquor and wine bottles. In the center of the room was a circular bar surrounded by orange Naugahyde stools. The bar stood about two feet below the level of the rest of the floor in a pit with a railing around it, broken at each quadrant by a small stairway. The bartender and his few patrons looked up at O'Rourke and Maurice without much interest as they entered, then went back to whatever they'd been doing before.

O'Rourke was beside himself. "If we do not stop for a drink in this peculiar place, we will regret it the rest of our lives. Allow me to buy you a cocktail, Maurice."

They descended into the pit and seated themselves at the bar. To their left, an attractive young woman wearing a frilly red blouse, tight designer jeans and high heels nursed a whiskey sour as she read from a paperback world almanac. Every now and then she found something amusing enough in the book to make her giggle.

Across the way sat three very short, old men who looked like retired jockeys. They were dressed with low rent flair, wide wing collars worn over the lapels of their garish polyester sport coats and lots of gold jewelry.

The seated patrons of Al's Discount Liquor were completed by two truck driver types with long hair, cowboy hats and tattoos. They had a bottle in a paper bag on the bar but they were drinking draft beer from the tap.

The heavyset bartender wore a black T-shirt and a green peaked cap. It was he who approached O'Rourke and Maurice and took their order.

"Two brandies," said O'Rourke, "to rekindle the embers and keep the home fire burning."

"Whatever you say, pal," said the bartender in a gravelly voice. "You're paying for the chair." He returned with two generous shots and set them down on the bar. "That'll be three-fifty," he said.

"Well, I certainly can't complain about the price structure around here," said O'Rourke as he handed the bartender a five.

"Everyone else does," said the bartender as he rang up the sale on the cash register and handed O'Rourke back his change. O'Rourke pushed the money back across the bar. The bartender looked at O'Rourke as if he dealing with a dangerous lunatic.

"Uh, all that's for me?"

"Most extraordinary," said O'Rourke to Maurice after he had convinced the bartender that the entire dollar and a half was meant as a tip. "These people are living on a level of currency exchange that passed us by thirty years ago."

The bartender returned from the other side of

the bar and spoke to the young woman. "Shiree, LeMoan wants to buy you a drink." The young woman looked up from her almanac.

"Who's LeMoan?" she said.

"One of those old fucks across the bar," the bartender growled.

Shiree flashed a brilliant smile. "I don't see anyone old around here," she said loudly. "Thank you so much."

The three old gents raised their glasses in a toast as Shiree simpered and ordered another whiskey sour.

"But which one is LeMoan?" said O'Rourke to Maurice. "Doesn't she care?"

"Would you? They all look like LeMoan from here," said Maurice.

"I don't know what to make of it," said O'Rourke. "but I suppose we must respect the mating rituals of alien cultures no matter how bizarre they seem."

Just as he spoke, another woman barreled through the double glass doors and headed purposefully toward the bar. In sharp contrast to Shiree, she was middle-aged, severely overweight and possessed of the sort of broad forehead that one usually associates with victims of Down's syndrome.

"LeMoan!" she barked. "You told me you were going to get the bottle and come right back!"

One of the old men at the bar turned and cringed at this onslaught. "Berthleen," he whined, "I'm just having one drink."

The truck drivers started snickering and Berthleen turned her wrath on them. "What the hell are you two idiots laughing at?" she demanded.

"I have a feeling this woman has a switchblade in her purse," O'Rourke said to Maurice. "Perhaps we should flee before the mayhem commences."

Having intimidated the truck drivers, Berthleen resumed berating LeMoan. "Hounding around with these low life friends of yours while I'm waiting outside! You told me you were getting the bottle and coming right back!"

"I believe you're right," said Maurice to O'Rourke.

They got up from their stools and climbed out of the pit to the main floor.

"Goddammit, Berthleen!" the bartender rumbled. "You come in here acting crazy and scare away my customers!"

"Customers!" Berthleen snorted. "That's what you call these shitbums?"

"Alright, that's it, I've had it!" the bartender roared as he took off his apron and came out into the pit to confront Berthleen.

Berthleen pulled a tiny, steel blue automatic from her purse and pointed it at him. "You take one more step, Mern Forgash, and I'll blow your head off! Don't think I don't mean it!"

"It's really none of my business," said Shiree pointedly, "but Mern is an awfully nice gentleman and I'd hate to see him get shot in his own bar."

"Jesus, Berthleen," LeMoan whined, "why do you have to embarrass me this way?"

"Why didn't you bring the bottle back!" Berthleen screeched.

O'Rourke and Maurice retreated out the double glass door into the foyer of the Happy Shopper and reconnoitered. Maurice almost doubled over with laughter.

"Your unwise wish to know how the locals spend the winter months has been granted," said O'Rourke. "I told you it was a bad idea."

"Don't you think we ought to report this to someone," Maurice gasped. "I mean, the woman's got a gun."

"The first rule of the serious cultural anthropologist is not to interfere with the native customs," said O'Rourke. "We might be tampering with the entire course of their social evolution."

They left the Happy Shopper without exploring the distressed canned goods and resumed their journey east. "I do fear that we are heading into a savage land," said O'Rourke. "The backward course of this frozen river can only lead us into a human wilderness which will shake all of our civilized assumptions to the core."

"Who you calling 'civilized', white man," Maurice guffawed. "I was just beginning to enjoy myself."

"You laugh now, Maurice. We shall see what form of expression you employ later on."

As O'Rourke spoke the sky darkened and the barren landscape seemed to merge with the firmament in one contiguous, leaden blur.

"I haven't seen such light since Venice," said O'Rourke, "where boats seem to float above your head in a sea of fog. Here it will be witches on brooms, no doubt."

On they drove through frozen fields and an occasional tiny hamlet with a gas station and a roadhouse. None of these looked particularly inviting and O'Rourke and Maurice did not stop until they came to a junction where they had to make a left turn to continue on to Glandville.

"We are close," said O'Rourke. "The hairs on the back of my neck are aroused and I feel something grotesque nearby, something that inhabits this land and all who enter into it."

"Would you knock it off," said Maurice. "You ought to be glad the trip is almost over."

"Half over," said O'Rourke darkly, "and we have not yet accomplished our purpose."

"I think you need a serious drink," said Maurice as he looked in the rearview mirror nervously. A huge radiator grill with a signature bulldog hood ornament was all he could see. "What's this truck riding our ass..." he muttered just as the tractor pulled out into the left lane and roared past them pulling a trailer with a huge, angular boulder chained down to its flat bed.

"Jesus! That motherfucker's in some kind of hurry," said Maurice.

"It is the raw substance of our desire," said O'Rourke, "being raced along to some Satanic mill where it will be cut and boxed and labeled. It is the very thing that has drawn us here, I fear."

They passed a series of roadside signs that advertised Norm's Furniture Barn, the Quarry Motel, and a restaurant called Clyde Feeley's Prime Rib ("Full Smorgasbord"). They passed a cluster of decrepit trailer homes with outhouses and wood smoke billowing from ramshackle stovepipe chimneys.

"Now there is a sight to behold," O'Rourke exclaimed. "Have I ever told you that it's always been my ambition to retire to such a community? I would get myself a couple of dogs, a Crag rifle, drink whiskey all day, and sniff around after large divorced women, the kind who are perpetually in pin curlers and possess an enormous generosity of spirit. I would find a place in their social structure as a sort of idiot savant, the old geezer whom the young, the barefoot, and the pregnant come to for sage advice on their poor marriage choices even though they generally agree that I am completely crazy. To corroborate their opinion I would construct some eccentric, primitive sculptures in my yard which, to my neighbors' astonishment, would one day be discovered by a big time New York gallery owner out in the boonies to do a little antiquing. People magazine would do a story on me, I would attend my opening as an authentic naif and amuse the collectors with stories of trout tickling and squirrel stew. The police would find me frozen solid on the Bowery the next morning with a crooked smile on my face and a pint bottle of Heaven Hill clutched in my aboriginal paw."

"It sounds like you're going to be pretty busy in your twilight years," said Maurice.

"Yes indeed," said O'Rourke. "You won't find these old hands idle. There are D-cups to unsnap, there is an artistic legacy to pass on."

They were now clearly on the outskirts of

Glandville. They passed a sign festooned with the insignias of the Rotary Club, the Lions, the Kiwanis, and the International Order of Odd Fellows that welcomed them to "The Slate Capitol of the World".

"We have arrived," said Maurice. "What do we do now?"

"We must search out the Kandeko slate mill, make our purchase and get out of this godforsaken place as quickly as possible," said O'Rourke, "but first we must fortify ourselves for that impending ordeal. Stop at the first emporium of fermented malt beverages that you see."

Maurice pulled the truck over into a Stewart's sandwich shop with two gas pumps outside. They went into the store, located a six-pack of Genesee Ale in the refrigerator and took it back to the counter. There was no one there but they could hear the sounds of an argument coming from somewhere in back.

"Hello!" O'Rourke called out. The argument stopped abruptly and a tiny woman, a dwarf actually, appeared to take care of their purchase. She was in her early twenties with dyed blonde hair and dark black roots. She smiled brilliantly.

"I'm sorry," she said, "I hope you haven't been waiting long."

"Oh no," said O'Rourke. "We only just arrived."

"It's so cold out there maybe you want me to warm this up in the microwave," she said and giggled.

"Kind of you to offer," said O'Rourke, "but we are trying to achieve equilibrium by bringing our interior temperature down to the frigid level of the weather. Could you perhaps tell us where the Kandeko slate mill is located?"

"Just about everywhere," said the girl. "They own this town. You just drive down the road another half mile or so and you'll see a big water tower on your right. That's what you're looking for."

Back in the truck, Maurice popped the top on a can of ale and said, "The natives seem friendly enough to me."

"Don't you know that midgets and microwaves are bad luck?" said O'Rourke. "We've got the whammy on for sure now."

They drove a short distance and the water tower came into view with KANDEKO spelled out in big, block letters across the tank. Beneath it was a huge corrugated aluminum shed surrounded by an unpaved yard dotted with massive boulders in a variety of colors – sea green, charcoal, rust red and dark purple. They turned off the road and fishtailed across the frozen ground to a stop outside the mill.

The place seemed abandoned except for the high-pitched whine of machinery that came from within.

"We are here," said O'Rourke. "Shall we pay a visit on those who shape raw stone from the earth into the pristine stuff of patios and steam room walls?"

They got out of the truck and headed for a door with the sign: KEEP OUT, Authorized Personnel Only. Through this they passed into one of the strangest places they had ever seen. The interior of the shed was pitch black except for faint, violet lights over the milling tables. Shadowy figures moved through a Stygian fog of water vapor thrown off by the cutting and shaping machines. The noise had the screeching, tooth grinding quality of fingernails scraping across a blackboard.

"I have seen many hellish places," O'Rourke shouted above the din, "but this really takes the cake!"

They walked over to the nearest table where an old man in a rain hat was grinding one side of an enormous slab smooth. Under the purple light, his pallor was ghastly white, the color of a grub under an overturned rock.

"Excuse me!" O'Rourke called out. "We're looking for the sales office!"

The old man looked up uncomprehendingly and waved them toward the entrance door. He led them back out of the shed into the yard.

"What's that you want?" he said.

"We're looking for the sales office," said O'Rourke.

"Oh, that's Mrs. Kandy you want to talk to," said the old man. "She's in that trailer down the hill." He pointed to a mobile home set on a cinder block foundation at the far end of the yard. "She'll fix you up alright," he said and chuckled cryptically.

O'Rourke thanked him and he and Maurice set out across the yard toward the trailer.

"The old coot's probably worked in that infernal place all his life. I'm surprised he can see or hear anything at all."

As they neared their destination, they began to make out some of its peculiar architectural features – faux brick siding, a very ornate, white, wrought iron railing around the porch, a cast iron, black jockey holding out a hitching ring, a garishly painted statue of the Virgin Mary standing in a stone niche, a concrete birdbath with an enormous green glass bulb sitting in its center, and planter boxes filled with plastic flowers all around the base of the cinder block foundation.

"The impulse to landscape," O'Rourke sighed, "is always poignant, no matter how fantastic the results."

They climbed the short stairway to the door and Maurice knocked. There was no immediate answer. He knocked again.

"Who's there?" a high, nasal voice barked from within.

"We're looking for Mrs. Kandy," O'Rourke responded.

"What do you want with her?" the voice shot back.

Maurice and O'Rourke exchanged a perplexed glance. "We're interested in buying some slate tile," said O'Rourke. "A man at the mill..."

The door opened suddenly and they were confronted by a middle-aged, dark haired woman in a pink fluffy sweater, a tight black skirt, and pink, fluffy slippers. She was not bad looking and wore far more make-up than she had to. Her mood was not cordial.

"What do you think this is?" she snapped. "K-Mart? We deal with distributors, we deal with major companies. Who are you anyway?"

"Allow me to introduce myself," said O'Rourke suavely. "My name is Robert O'Rourke and I represent Rocket Tile in New York city. This is my assistant, Maurice."

"You look like a couple of floor apes to me," said the woman, "and you're not scratching up this tree."

"I assure you, madame . . ." O'Rourke resumed before the door was slammed in his face. "Was it something I said?" he asked Maurice.

"You didn't say much," said Maurice.

O'Rourke was annoyed. He knocked on the door and called out, "We've driven all the way from New York, Mrs. Kandy. We want to make a substantial purchase and we have cash to pay for it."

"If you don't get off my property," came the response, "I'm going to call the police!"

"Police?!" O'Rourke was aghast.

"Come on," said Maurice, "let's get out of here."

"Whatever happened to the free market?" O'Rourke fumed as Maurice preceded him back toward the parked truck, "the very bulwark of the hideous American way of life! I offer that bitch cash and she threatens me with the heat! The woman must be some kind of lunatic!"

"What do we do now?" said Maurice.

"We buy the fucking slate somewhere else," O'Rourke growled. "That cranky cunt can't be the only game in town."

Maurice turned the truck around and drove out onto the road.

"You see that neon sign down to the left?" said

O'Rourke. "Let's drive down there and ask some questions. Jesus, am I pissed off!"

The establishment with the neon sign turned out to be Clyde Feeley's Prime Rib, which boasted a cocktail lounge with its own entrance separate from the dining room. The floor was an ugly pattern of different color slate tiles and the walls were covered with photographs of quarry operations and men in hardhats standing next to outcrops and heavy machinery. It was at the bar of this lounge that O'Rourke and Maurice sat down to review their prospects.

"Excuse me," said O'Rourke to the bartender after they'd ordered ham sandwiches and a couple of whiskeys, "we are in the market for a quantity of slate tile. Could you tell us where we might find it?"

"There's only one place to go," said the bartender. "That's Kandeko right down the road here."

"We've already been," said O'Rourke, "and we met with a less than enthusiastic reception."

The bartender chuckled. "I guess you must have run into Connie Kandy. She's a formidable woman."

"You're telling me," said O'Rourke. "That can't possibly be the only slate mill around here though."

"Oh no, there's a couple more," said the bartender, "but she owns them too. Nothing moves in this town without her say-so."

"Why won't she sell to us? We were willing to

pay cash for a considerable load."

"I won't even venture a guess on that one, friend. She's got a crazy way of thinking that no one can figure out. She's one tough cookie, though. The woman's already buried two rich husbands – just ground them down into slurry like a water grinder." He wiped down the bar and casually asked, "How much slate were you looking for?"

"Seventy-five boxes," said O'Rourke.

The bartender whistled. "That's some weight. Any particular color?"

O'Rourke's antennae immediately picked up the bartender's new tone – simultaneously diffident and conspiratorial. "Green," he replied.

"It's a shame you guys drive all the way from New York city in this weather for nothing," said the bartender as he poured them two more drinks. "These are with me." Then he walked to the other end of the bar and picked up the phone. His minute long conversation was inaudible to O'Rourke and Maurice but the bartender looked pleased by what he heard. He hung up and rejoined his two patrons.

"You know," he said, "I might just be able to help you guys out."

"How's that?" said O'Rourke.

"Friend of mine works in one of the mills and he says he can get what you want. We just got to be quiet about it."

"We are grateful for your assistance," said O'Rourke, "and we shall exercise the utmost discretion in the matter."

The price the bartender quoted was even less than O'Rourke had expected to pay at the mill. "This stuff must be hot," he asided to Maurice, "but we are in no position to travel the moral high road."

The bartender told them that he had arranged a rendezvous with a man called Henry at a farm about five miles down the road.

"It's not a working farm anymore but it's got a barn and a silo and a rundown old white house. There's a sign out front on the road that says: 'Grizmold'. You just show up with the cash and Henry's got what you want right there."

"I don't know how to thank you," said O'Rourke as they paid their tab and got up to leave.

"Don't you worry about me," said the bartender. "Henry's picking up my end. Just be sure you don't mention this to anyone."

"Clearly a man with an eye for the main chance," said O'Rourke as he and Maurice got back into the truck.

"He makes it sound as if we're picking up a load of cocaine."

"Turn up the heat," said Maurice.

They drove back down the highway out of Glandville proper and eventually spotted

"Grizmold" painted on a teetering mailbox by the roadside. The house was down in a gully and, from the look of the peeling white paint on its exterior, appeared to have been abandoned for years. Further down the ravine, a decrepit barn and a collapsing silo leaned against each other like two drunks trying to hold each other up.

"We have arrived," said O'Rourke as they cautiously negotiated the slippery driveway that led down to the house. They parked the truck next to an ancient washing machine with a mangle lying on its side in the yard and cased the joint from the vantage of the cab.

"There doesn't seem to be anybody home," O'Rourke observed.

"I don't think anyone's been home in quite some time," said Maurice.

"Let's take a look around," O'Rourke suggested. "We may be early."

They left the truck and crunched through the snow to the front door of the house. O'Rourke knocked. There was no response. He knocked again and called out, "Hello! Is anybody in there?!"

"Stop that yelling!" a voice hissed.

O'Rourke and Maurice whirled around and saw an old man in a heavy, red plaid jacket and a blue wool cap gesturing at them angrily from the side of the house. "Follow me," he said and headed off at a brisk pace toward the barn.

O'Rourke and Maurice hurried to catch up with him. "Are you Henry?" said O'Rourke.

"The same," said the old man.

"I am Robert O'Rourke and this is Maurice."

"I don't want to know your names," the old man snapped.

They came to the barn and the old man pulled back the weather-beaten, wooden door, which rolled on little wheels along a rusty rail and made a screeching sound that set O'Rourke's few real teeth on edge. Inside the barn, it was dank and sharply musty; in the summer, the smell would be unendurable. Along one wall were stacks of foot square, cardboard boxes, six inches deep, the standard packaging for gauged slate tile.

"What was the color?" said the old man.

"Green," said O'Rourke.

"And that was seventy-five boxes you wanted. Send the boy to get the truck and you and me, we'll do some business," said the old man.

"You heard him, Maurice. Just back it up to the door."

Maurice did as he was told. The old man pointed to the stacked boxes and said, "There's the slate. Where's the money?"

"Right here," said O'Rourke and pulled a wad of twenties out of his pocket. "You want to count it?"

"I don't think that will be necessary," said Henry and it suddenly occurred to O'Rourke that the old man had been holding a rather large revolver in his hand for the last few seconds of their transaction. "Hand it over."

"Of course," said O'Rourke disgustedly. "I should have known what to expect in this hospitable little town."

"We like it," said the old man with a sly smile. He took the money from O'Rourke and ordered, "Turn around and put your hands behind your back."

"I will do no such thing," said O'Rourke. "You've got the money. Why don't you just take it and go."

The old man looked at him and chuckled. It was not a pleasant sound. "You must think I'm playing around," he said. "You just do what I say and maybe you and your friend live another day. You don't . . . "

There was something in the old man's voice that chilled O'Rourke. He might get shot if he cooperated. He would certainly get shot if he didn't. He turned and put his hands behind his back and the old man bound them together with the plastic strip riot police use to handcuff their captives. The truck was now slowly backing up to the open barn door.

"I thought you'd see it my way," said the old man. "I'm sure the young fellow will too."

As indeed Maurice did when he walked into the barn. He was duly trussed up and made to stand next to O'Rourke facing the wall.

"Don't either of you move a muscle for the next ten minutes," the old man warned. "It's been a pleasure doing business with you."

"Likewise, I'm sure," O'Rourke grumbled and the old man was gone. "I feel vaguely idiotic," he said to Maurice.

"You feel idiotic now," said Maurice, "take a look at this." He was peering through the slit opening between the barn door and the jamb. O'Rourke joined him and saw the old man climb into a maroon Cadillac on the road driven by Connie Kandy. The car then roared off in the direction of Glandville.

"We are not only boobs," said O'Rourke, "we are world class chumps. These hicks have taken us to the cleaners."

"Look," said Maurice, "we have more company." An old pick-up truck had turned off the road and was lurching down the driveway toward the barn.

"Probably the scavengers who strip the truck for parts," said O'Rourke. "We'll be lucky to get out of here with our shoes."

The pick-up came to a stop in front of the rental truck and a fat guy in a heavy ski parka and rubber boots got out.

"Halloo!" he called.

O'Rourke and Maurice looked at each other. Maurice shrugged as best he could with his hands tied behind his back. "Well, what's one more yorp in the cavalcade?" said O'Rourke. They walked out the open door of the barn and presented themselves to the new arrival.

"Hi, there," he said, "I'm Henry."

"We're obliged to take your word for it," said O'Rourke, "but Henry seems to be a rather common name around these parts."

"Jeez," said Henry, "what in hell happened to you?"

"Just get us loose and we'll tell you all about it." Henry cut through their plastic ties with a large folding knife and became more and more agitated as they told him their story.

"So this old guy just tied you up and left?" he demanded.

"That's right," said O'Rourke. "We saw him get into a car with Connie Kandy and drive off."

Henry's face turned ashen. "Connie Kandy?! Jesus Christ! Why didn't you say so in the first place!" He started tearing off the tops of the slate cartons. They were all filled with dirt. "Damn! I got to get out of here!" He raced out the door, jumped in his pick-up, and took off.

"I guess it's every man for himself in Glandville," said O'Rourke. "We better follow Henry's example and make our own hasty exit."

"We've got to call the police," said Maurice.

"I don't think our complaint would fall on sympathetic ears," said O'Rourke. "A leading member of the community who assists in armed robberies obviously has some influence with the local constabulary. I, for one, do not wish to be beaten about the head and ears with truncheons, thrown in a cell and ejected from town early tomorrow morning as a vagrant. I think that is about as much as we could expect from the Glandville police."

"We can't just let her get away with this!" Maurice sputtered.

"I'm afraid she already has," said O'Rourke.

"What can possibly be going through your mind? Do you want to take on the entire population of this hellhole in a crusade for honesty and fair play? Do you think you can cow these savages with the sword of justice?"

"Why don't we burn down her trailer?"

"Oh, shit," said O'Rourke. "You really are trying to keep an appointment in Glandville. Get in that truck and do as I say." Maurice fishtailed out of the icy driveway and O'Rourke pointed south.

"We have seen many things today," said O'Rourke, "and I have no desire to see any more. With our tails firmly clenched between our legs, we bid adieu to the fine citizens of Glandville. We can only hope that their quarrying operations open a hole to the center of the earth and the town is inundated in a huge eruption of flaming magma."

A Woman Scorned

4

"Goddammit!" master tile mason Robert O'Rourke bellowed as the piece of marble he was trying to set cracked cleanly along a fault line. "What am I doing in this place?"

"You are here to do a job of work," said his assistant Maurice.

"I don't mean this shithouse, I mean the planet," said O'Rourke as he pried the two pieces of broken tile out of the mastic on the floor. "There is some malignant god up there who wishes to see us broken and humiliated. It is either Poseidon, the god of plumbing, or Eris, the goddess of domestic squabbles. We must make a proper sacrifice to palliate them. Pour that whiskey down the toilet."

Maurice was aghast. "Have you lost your mind?!"

"Very probably," said O'Rourke. "This place is driving me crazy."

The place in question was a small powder room in the Park Avenue apartment of Al Shallot and his wife Bijou. O'Rourke and Maurice had previously tiled the restrooms in the office suite of Shallot's printing business and behaved rather badly on the job, joking and flirting with the secretaries, going to lunch for two hours and coming back with a load on, ignoring the nervous admonitions of the junior executives, and even making loud fun of Shallot himself. Throughout the few days they were there, Shallot, who thought of himself as a real no-nonsense kind of guy, must have been on the constant verge of exploding in rage. O'Rourke and Maurice were utterly baffled when he called a week after they'd left and offered them a job in his very own apartment.

"The man is up to no good," O'Rourke muttered as he hung up the phone. "He is either insane or a masochist. Perhaps he intends to bump us off in the privacy of his posh domicile."

But this was not the case. When they arrived, Shallot introduced them to his wife as if they were master artisans. "The best in their field," he said without evident irony.

Bijou Shallot, who was five feet tall, thin as a rail, pinched as a squeezed lemon and dry as a prune, oohed and aahed to be in the presence of such exalted craftsmen. "I know you're going to do a wonderful job," she cooed. It was the last time they would hear a civil word from her mouth.

The first thing Mrs. Shallot did was insist that they make a totally improper installation in order to save money. "I saw them do it on 'This Old House'."

"But, Mrs. Shallot," O'Rourke smoothly countered, "it would not be a good idea to set marble tile on this surface. You need a cement pad underneath."

"There will be no cement work in this house," snapped Mrs. Shallot. "We have a very valuable collection of paintings and the dust would surely do them damage."

It was finally decided that they would pull up the vinyl tile that was on the floor and glue the marble to whatever was underneath. Mrs. Shallot made it clear that any other suggestion would be treated as a brazen attempt to jack up the price and she was not about to get taken off by a couple of lowly tradesmen.

The next day, O'Rourke and Maurice returned with their tools and enough white Carrara to do the job. Al and Bijou Shallot were taking their breakfast, seated at a tiny, sunlit table pushed up against a pair of French doors and ignored the tilemen until they brought in their water saw.

"What on earth!" Mrs. Shallot exclaimed. "You're not bringing that thing in my house!"

O'Rourke tried to explain that it was the only way they could cut the marble.

"You will remove that machine from this apartment immediately," said Mrs. Shallot coldly. "You can find a place for it in the basement." O'Rourke caught Al smirking.

"The man has set us up!" he sputtered to Maurice as they descended in the elevator with the water saw. "His horror show wife is the agent of his revenge."

The Dominican elevator man laughed. "That lady very difficult."

"Difficult for you as well, my good man," said O'Rourke. "We shall have to command the elevator for each cut that we make. Jesus, what a pain in the ass!"

And their problems were only beginning. When they pulled up the vinyl tile, they discovered that it had been set in Bulldog mastic – thick, gooey, black adhesive.

"We can't possibly glue down the tile on this surface," said O'Rourke. "The black stuff will leech right through the marble."

Mrs. Shallot was not of the same mind. "I know exactly what you're up to and you're not going to get away with it. Set that marble exactly as I told you."

"There are only two options," said O'Rourke. "We can set the floor on fire and burn the shit off or we can throw in a bucket of shellac and try to seal it up. The former would probably be more effective but I doubt that Mrs. Shallot would see it that way."

So shellac it was. They painted on three thick coats and began setting. At first, this dubious procedure seemed to work. Cutting was ridiculously time consuming because of the distance Maurice had to travel to the water saw, but no stains appeared on the surface of the marble and O'Rourke was of the opinion, "We just might get away with this."

"Did I ever tell you the story of why my ex-wife divorced me?" said O'Rourke as he fit another tile into place.

"I believe I've heard a few different versions," said Maurice.

"The poor woman did have a number of reasons, Lord knows, but there was one thing in particular that pushed her right over the edge. I can still remember being wakened by her in the middle of the night and accused of some misdeed that I had committed. 'You just left me there!' she wailed. 'Where? What are you talking about?' I protested in my bleary state. 'Out in the desert! You just drove off and left me there!'

"This specificity gave me pause. When had we been in the desert together? Was there something I'd forgotten?"

"Probably her birthday," said Maurice.

"I always forgot that," said O'Rourke. "No, it was something she'd just dreamed. 'You've been dreaming,' I pointed out reasonably. It did no good. 'You're a louse,' she moaned, then rolled over and went back to sleep. I thought nothing of it at the time but that was only the beginning.

"A week later I dreamed I was very small and I was being beaten by my father for reasons I could not understand. It was especially terrifying because my father had never beaten me before. I woke up in an agony of fear and confusion and discovered that I actually was being beaten, not by my father but my wife. 'How could you do that to me?!' she shrieked as she pummeled me.

"I staggered out of bed and bellowed 'Have you lost your mind, woman?!" She paid no attention. 'With my own best friend!,' she bawled. 'When I'm finished with you I'll tear that bitch's hair out!'

" 'Would you mind telling me what I've done?' I demanded.

" 'You've been fucking Marie!'

"I was flabbergasted by this accusation. Marie was

not bad looking and we had just enough hostility toward each other to make a good boff interesting, but we had never even come close. 'I have never fucked Marie,' I protested. 'Don't tell me that,' she replied. 'You were just doing it. In my dream.'

" 'Listen,' I said, 'you stay out of my dreams and I'll try to stay out of yours'. It was not the right thing to say. 'Is that what you think of me?' she demanded. 'Is that how little I mean to you?'

"Now, you know, Maurice, that the male of the species simply cannot win this sort of argument. It isn't about anything anyway. Or, more accurately, it's about everything but the subject at hand. I wisely quit the field and went to the kitchen for a beer. By the time I returned to the bedroom, she had gone back to sleep but I was still leery of rejoining her at close proximity and possibly precipitating another attack. I spent the rest of the night on the couch and slept like a baby.

"The next morning, she demanded to know why I had abandoned the marriage bed. 'Am I that repulsive to you?' she lamented. 'No, of course not,' I replied and recapitulated the events of the previous evening which had driven me from her side. 'Who knows what you were going to dream next? I was afraid for my life,' I joked.

"This riposte cheered her immensely. 'Really?' she said. 'I like that idea.'

"Well, things went from bad to worse. The crimes I committed while she was in the embrace of Morpheus escalated to the monstrous and unspeakable. I blush when I think of them. She finally threw me out. I suppose I deserved it after all I'd done. I mean, does it really matter whether you torture people in their dreams or the so-called waking state?

"I took up residence in my present humble abode and brooded through the next several months. It is terrible to be a creature of habit, Maurice. My dependence on this woman who had brought me little but irritation and an occasional discharge of lustful tension came as a shock to me. It preyed on my mind. It followed me everywhere and disrupted my whole day to day existence. The simplest functions became daunting and painful. The damn woman was living in my head and she refused to be evicted."

"Ah," said Maurice, "what is this thing called love?"

"I'll tell you what it is," said O'Rourke. "It's a goddam pain in the ass. But it keeps people together. Even people who hate each other. Take Al and Bijou. What possible motive could they have for cohabiting?"

"It looks like a purely sexual relationship to me," said Maurice and laughed.

"Can you imagine those two locked like rutting beasts in connubial embrace?" said O'Rourke. "It gives me the shakes. No, I'm sure Al's taste runs to liberal-minded call girls whom he pays large sums of money to commit loathsome and unimaginably degrading acts on his person. Embittered Bijou has been left in the churning wake of life and contents herself with making things hard for everyone else. If she was an Eskimo, they would have set her adrift on an ice floe years ago."

"Can it," Maurice warned. "I hear footsteps." Bijou Shallot appeared at the door of the powder room and stared down at O'Rourke on the floor. She stood a moment and said nothing, then walked away.

"The woman certainly has a way of making her presence felt," O'Rourke muttered. "The back of my neck is burning from the microwave energy she puts out. Speaking of which, it is time for lunch. Let us flee this unhappy home for the convivial surroundings of the local low rent bar and grill."

They left the Shallot apartment and dawdled through a long lunch hour at the Pearl of Erin on

Lexington Avenue over steam table corned beef, bourbon and beer.

When they returned, they found Bijou Shallot standing at the door of the powder room. She pointed at the floor. "What... is... that?" she demanded, emphasizing each word. O'Rourke looked down at the black stains leeching through two of the tiles under the pedestal sink.

"Nothing we can't fix," he replied smoothly. "Happens all the time. We will pull up the defective pieces and replace them."

"Thank you, Bob," she said sourly, turned on her heel and walked off.

"Begab," said O'Rourke, "we are undone. I can already see the outlines of a lawsuit in the offing."

"It's not our fault," said Maurice. "We told her not to set marble on that stuff."

"We must act quickly," said O'Rourke. "Break out those tiles and get me the shellac. We can only pray that the problem is localized and that the rest of the floor will last long enough for the check to clear."

They worked feverishly for the rest of the afternoon, sealing, cutting, setting and grouting. When the floor was done, O'Rourke solicited and obtained Bijou Shallot's approval and requested the final payment.

"I will have to get a check from Al," she said. "You can pick it up tomorrow."

"We are fucked," said O'Rourke sadly to Maurice in the elevator they descended. "It will be a miracle if the whole thing doesn't turn black by tomorrow."

The next morning they returned with much trepidation and found the Shallots breakfasting at their little table by the window.

"I want to talk to you, Bob," said Bijou with enough severity to frighten O'Rourke into an immediate defensive posture.

"I don't really see how you can blame – " he started to say but she cut him off.

"I have a friend who is renovating her kitchen. I would appreciate it if you could give her an estimate."

O'Rourke was confounded. "Well, I, uh, we're pretty busy..."

"I told her you would drop by her apartment after I gave you your check. She lives right down the block."

"Yes, of course," said O'Rourke. Al Shallot, who lived in the cool, crystal air of utter contempt for his fellow man, betrayed his pleasure in O'Rourke's discomfort with only the slightest of smiles.

"What are we going to do now?" O'Rourke fumed as they walked out of the building. "We are getting sucked into a quagmire by that bastard."

"What's the problem?" said Maurice. "We got paid and we got another job."

"Don't you see?" O'Rourke sputtered. "Suppose that marble turns black when we are half done with Bijou's friend's kitchen. We willed be sued by the Shallots and fired by the friend. That sonuvabitch is out to get us!"

"Don't be so paranoid," said Maurice. "The marble looked fine and we're out of work."

"Alright, Maurice, but don't say I didn't tell you so when the shit hits the fan. Against my better judgment we will go look at the job."

And that is how they met Carlotta Coll. Dressed as badly as they were, the doorman still sent them up the wood-paneled elevator off the front entrance and Mrs. Coll herself answered the door. She was a tall, blond woman in her early fifties, just beginning to put on weight. She had certainly been a looker in her time and her vanity had not diminished. She was made up as if she were hosting a cocktail party.

"I'm so glad Bijou sent you over," she said after they'd exchanged introductions. "My daughter is coming to stay with me for two weeks and I absolutely have to have the kitchen done by then."

"We shall endeavor to adhere to your schedule," O'Rourke reassured her.

"Wonderful," she said. "Would you like a drink?"

O'Rourke and Maurice were slightly taken aback. It was only ten thirty in the morning and, although they often started drinking much earlier than that, they were surprised to find a kindred spirit in a Park Avenue matron like Mrs. Coll.

"Perhaps we should look at the kitchen first," O'Rourke suggested.

"Of course!" Mrs. Coll whinnied. "What can I be thinking?" They went into the kitchen and discovered that it was in much the same condition as the Shallot powder room. Linoleum had been stripped off the concrete floor and the black adhesive had dried into a hard, dusty crust.

"This stuff will all have to be chipped up," said O'Rourke.

"Of course, whatever you say," said Mrs. Coll. "Do you do that sort of work?"

"Yes, we do," said O'Rourke. "It's not much fun but it's got to be done."

Mrs. Coll described the tiles she wanted – six inch, white hexagonal – and they agreed on a price, a rather high price. O'Rourke's instinct told him that money was probably not an object with this woman and he was right.

"When can you start?" she asked.

"Right away, if it's convenient," O'Rourke replied.

"Convenient? God is it ever!" she said with such enthusiasm you might have thought she'd just won the lottery. "Now, how about that drink?" She led them into the study and made them each a bourbon and water. She had gin martini herself.

"Thank you so much for doing this on such short notice," she said. "I can't tell you how much I appreciate it."

"It's no problem, Mrs. Coll," said O'Rourke.

"Please, call me Carlotta. I'm a very informal person. I hope that doesn't bother you."

"Not at all," said O'Rourke graciously and thought he caught the slightest trace of a leer flash across Mrs. Coll's painted face. He and Maurice finished their drinks and departed shortly thereafter.

"I'm afraid you'll have to take the service entrance from now on," said Mrs. Coll apologetically. "The people in this building really have a stick up their –" She caught herself and giggled at her own coyness. "Well, they just wouldn't approve if I had you in through the front door."

"Most extraordinary," said O'Rourke once he and Maurice were out on the street. "I find it difficult to believe that this brazen woman is a friend of Bijou Shallot."

"This woman is trouble," said Maurice.

"All women are trouble," O'Rourke rejoined. "Hasn't spending your life in their kitchens and bathrooms taught you that? Be of good cheer and let us repair to Mrs. Coll's bank where I will cash this check. What ever the immediate future holds for us, this cash, at least, is ours."

The next morning, O'Rourke and Maurice assembled tools and tile and vanned them up to the service entrance of Mrs. Coll's building. They rang the buzzer to the rear door of her apartment and were surprised when she answered herself, clad in a blue satin dressing gown with a feather collar.

"Come in, come in," she gushed. "How nice to see you." She had not just popped out of bed. Her hair and nails were lacquered; an aura of sweet fragrance clung about her in a cloying effluvium. She was also completely looped.

"If there's anything I can do to help, just give a holler," she said and left them in the kitchen.

"It is only nine thirty and the woman is already

shitfaced," O'Rourke marveled. "Maybe she will pass out and afford us an opportunity to rifle through her belongings. I'm sure there must be a few items of interest around here."

They loaded their materials into a large closet off the service corridor and set to work with hammers and cold chisels on the dry black mastic that covered the floor. It was slow going.

"I hate this shit," Maurice complained. "It will take us forever to get all this stuff up."

"Two days is a rather peculiar way to look at eternity," O'Rourke observed. "You are caught up in the apparent relativity of time. Due to the tedium of the task, each second you spend chipping away at this floor seems like a minute, each minute an hour, each hour a day. Time stretches before you like a vast and hostile desert that confounds your crossing to the oasis on the horizon. Who knows? It's probably a mirage anyway. You want to give up, you want to lie down, bury yourself in the sand and shut out the whole ugly, arid world. Why keep going? Why do anything? The utter futility –"

"Alright, alright," Maurice interrupted. "Cut the bullshit and throw me a beer."

"Ah yes, the medicaments," said O'Rourke reaching into his canvas tool bag. "A flagon of mead is what we need."

And so they chipped, on through the morning into the early afternoon. When they decided to leave for lunch, Mrs. Coll did not respond to O'Rourke's shouted advisement that they would return within the hour.

"She is most certainly down for the count," O'Rourke surmised.

Immediately outside the service entrance, a demolition crew that looked like refugees from a pirate ship or a Bosch painting was busy emptying rolling containers into a garbage hauler. The radiator grill of the truck was festooned with a shattered mannequin head held in place by criss-crossing lengths of frayed, heavy rope. O'Rourke was charmed by this grotesque and disturbing totem.

"Art is not dead after all," he said and waved to the Puerto Rican driver who returned a thumbs up signal. "I do not envy that man's wife, however. Keep up the good work!!," he shouted out over the din of clanging metal, grunting, cursing laborers, and the compactor motor.

They repaired to lunch at small diner frequented by the building maintenance people from that opulent neighborhood, ate their indifferent burgers and fries, and soon returned to Mrs. Coll's service entrance which O'Rourke had left unlocked to assure their re-entry.

One can imagine their astonishment when they opened the door and found Mrs. Coll, still more or less in her dressing gown, seated on the floor with legs splayed to afford a clear view of her luxuriant pelt, chipping away at the black stuff with hammer and chisel.

"Mrs. Coll!" said aghast O'Rourke. "What on earth are you doing?"

"I'm helping you guys out," Mrs. Coll slurred without interrupting her good work. "And please, call me Carlotta."

"I'm sure that's very kind," said O'Rourke, "but there's really no need for your assistance."

"I like to get into things, get my hands dirty," Mrs. Coll replied. "Besides, I'm bored. I need some company."

O'Rourke and Maurice, at a loss for words, exchanged a panicked glance. Should they simply turn and flee? Was Mrs. Coll so far gone she would not remember the incident?

"Leonard never let me do anything like this," Mrs. Coll continued. "He was such a stuffed shirt."

"Leonard?" said O'Rourke.

"My ex-husband," said Mrs. Coll. "He drove me

crazy." She looked up at O'Rourke and her face sagged. "But I still love him . . . No, that's not true. I hate him!" Tears rolled down her cheeks and she started to blubber. "If I could just get my hands on that floozy who wrecked my marriage –" She fell back sobbing on the floor. Her parted robe left nothing to the imagination.

O'Rourke and Maurice stood there like a couple of gawking rubes at the carnival, struck dumb by this recumbent display of female flesh. Mrs. Coll was no spring chicken but she had the body of a thirty year old.

"Leonard!" she wailed. "How could you leave me like this?"

O'Rourke tried to take charge of the situation. "Mrs. Coll, you've –"

"Carlotta!" she howled.

"Carlotta," O'Rourke stood corrected, "you've got to get a grip on yourself. Let me help you up." He offered her his hands and she grabbed on. She did not try to stand, however.

"Leonard?" she said squinting through her rheumy eyes.

"No, it's me," said O'Rourke. "I'm –" With a startling exhibition of upper arm strength, Mrs. Coll quite suddenly pulled stout O'Rourke off balance right down on top of her. "Don't leave me, Leonard," she moaned. "Fuck me." She writhed in sexual abandon under the flabbergasted tileman.

"Mrs. Coll!" he roared. "I'm not Leonard!" He disengaged himself from her clench and scrambled to his feet.

Mrs. Coll looked up at him from the floor. "No, you're not, are you?" she said sadly. "Leonard was real man." She slowly got to her feet, pulled the dressing gown tightly around her and shuffled out of the room.

"Jesus Christ!" said Maurice. "What do we do now?"

"Punt," said O'Rourke. "You know, if you hadn't been standing there to inhibit me, I just might have done the woman's bidding."

"Remember the rules," said Maurice. "Never fuck the help, never fuck the boss, and never, ever fuck the client until the last check clears."

"You are, of course, absolutely correct," said O'Rourke, "but I am not likely to run into such a cooperative and well-preserved woman of this vintage again."

"I think we better retire from the field for the day," said Maurice. "You are clearly suffering some kind of overload."

"Only kidding," said O'Rourke. "We've got to get this black stuff up before Carlotta returns to render further service as a floor scraper." They worked with hectic speed through the afternoon and actually managed to finish three quarters of the job. Mrs. Coll did not reappear and they quietly let themselves out at the end of the day without informing her of their departure.

"We can only pray that tomorrow presents us with a less interesting situation," said O'Rourke. If anyone deserved to have a prayer not answered, it was O'Rourke, creature of blasphemy, and the events of the next day might even be construed to confirm the existence of the cantankerous, wrathful God of our Puritan forebears.

The two tilemen arrived at eight the next morning and could not raise anyone to let them into the apartment. The building superintendent was dubious about letting them use his passkey but finally relented to O'Rourke's hectoring. Hunkered down in the kitchen with a short can of Bud apiece, they debated the wisdom of trying to inform Mrs. Coll of their presence.

"He who steps from this room in search of Carlotta enters into a labyrinth from which no man returns," O'Rourke intoned.

"If we don't tell her we're here, she might think we're burglars or something," Maurice argued. "She might call the police."

"Don't be absurd," said O'Rourke. "When she hears the ring of hammer striking chisel she will know it is only us, toiling away at our craft." Any argument was rendered moot as Mrs. Coll, clad in her dressing gown, swept into the kitchen with the force of a cyclone.

"Who are you?! What are you doing in my kitchen?!" she demanded. There was a tense silence as O'Rourke and Maurice waited for Mrs. Coll to recognize them. "Well?!" she barked.

All that O'Rourke could think to say was, "We are here to tile your floor, Mrs. Coll."

"Carlotta!" she shrieked. "Never Mrs. Coll! Carlotta!

With that, she turned and stormed out of the room.

"Al Shallot certainly knew what he was doing when he set us up with this one," O'Rourke muttered sourly.

"What do we do now?" said Maurice.

"Nothing," said O'Rourke. "We continue working as if the incident never occurred. We are, after all, only employees and the bizarre behavior of those who pay us is none of our business."

"I have a sinking feeling that she's about to make it our business," said Maurice.

"Who was the one who got us into this ridiculous situation in the first place?" O'Rourke reproved. "And who was the one who sounded a word of warning?"

Suddenly, shouting erupted from the far reaches of the apartment.

"It sounds like two women but I can't make out what they're saying," said O'Rourke as he pressed his ear to the door. He did not have to wait long to find out.

Bijou Shallot, dressed in a red suit, came storming into the kitchen with Mrs. Coll close at her heels.

"You!" she said, pointing at O'Rourke. "You will pay for what you did to my powder room!"

"Leave him alone!" Mrs. Coll shrieked. "Leave my Leonard alone!"

Mrs. Shallot turned her wrath on her friend. "Shut up, you drunken slut! I'll deal with you after I've finished with these swindlers!"

O'Rourke nervously fingered a hammer that was lying on the counter and Maurice edged toward the service door.

"If you think you're going to get away – !" Mrs. Shallot's advance was stopped by a mighty blow to the back of her head from Mrs. Coll. She crumpled to the floor in a diminutive heap.

"I love you, Leonard!" Mrs. Coll wailed. "I did it for you, you crummy bastard!" She broke down sobbing over the prostrate form of Bijou Shallot.

O'Rourke and Maurice did not tarry. They grabbed as many tools as they could throw in a bag in a few seconds and raced out the back door. They did not bother ringing for the elevator but opted for the stairwell where their receding footsteps echoed up the shaft and combined with Mrs. Coll's lamentations, squalling from the interior of the apartment. Eleven stories below, the tilemen hit the street on a dead run and did not pull up until they were safely around the corner.

"My God!" O'Rourke gasped. "This material witness business does not agree with me at all! Do you suppose she killed the little bitch?"

"I hope so," said Maurice. "It would certainly solve a few of our problems."

"At least we'll get three squares a day in protective custody," said O'Rourke.

"I don't think it will come to that," said Maurice. "It would take more than getting whupped upside the head to take that one out."

"You've got a point," said O'Rourke. "Al Shallot, the grand engineer of this whole fiasco, is not going to get off that easy."

"What fiasco?" said Maurice. "We got some money and we never have to go back."

"The Shallot woman will have us in court," said

O'Rourke. "Of that I have no doubt."

"Who cares?" said Maurice. "We are not collectable. Besides, she would lose. We only did exactly what she told us."

"Right and wrong are irrelevant concepts if the plaintiff is wealthy. She will win the case and pursue us like a hound from hell."

"She wouldn't waste the time," Maurice scoffed. "The other one I'm not so sure about. She's really got the hots for you."

"Don't make light of the situation, Maurice. A woman in love may be twice as dangerous as a woman with a shitty tile job."

5
O'Rourke Gets Recessed

Master tile mason Robert O'Rourke looked at the unblinking answering machine in the tiny office of Rocket Tile, shook his head sadly, and turned to his assistant Maurice. "They don't call, they don't write," he said, "which reminds me of a story about an old Jewish woman and a gorilla."

"I've heard it," said Maurice.

"I imagine you have. It seems we have joined the ranks of the hardcore unemployables. I can't remember when we last had a job."

"Three weeks ago," said Maurice, "the shower repair on Barrow Street."

"Ah, yes, the horror of it all comes back to me now. Degrading ourselves for that kind of chump change."

"I'd be glad to degrade myself at this point," said Maurice. "If only I knew how."

"Don't take that attitude," O'Rourke admonished. "We've gone through slow times before. I mean, just because the whole economy is shot and the government is in the hands of a bunch of slavish lackeys toadying to a gang of rapacious criminals doesn't mean things can't turn around and allow a dishonest man to work for an honest day's pay. Just because the Guatemalization of the country is accelerating at a dizzying pace doesn't mean there aren't still a few opportunities available to the energetic sociopath. Take heart and pass me a beer."

Maurice handed O'Rourke a can of Minx stout malt liquor, but he did not take heart. "Maybe we should consider another line of business," he said sourly.

"That's easy for you to say," said O'Rourke. "You're young. You could probably get a job selling shoes. You could take a course in air conditioning repair. You might even be a gigolo. But what about me? What are the prospects for a fat, old fart like myself who has spent half his life on his hands and knees installing little ceramic squares behind toilets?"

"Well, we can't just sit here waiting for the phone to ring."

"How right you are, Maurice. Time and tide wait for no man. We must hit the streets and hustle up some employment. We may, perhaps, even be able to create our own job, as the entrepreneurs say. It is only a matter of carving out a niche in the market."

"You have been watching too many con men on late night TV," said Maurice.

"I do reserve a special place in my heart for those electronic purveyors of dreams," O'Rourke agreed, "but I think I'm capable of separating the wheat from the chaff. Occasionally, a golden grain can be gleaned from the most transparent of frauds."

"Do you have something in mind?" said Maurice warily.

"Indeed I do," said O'Rourke, "drink up and follow me out into a world where the man of nerve and imagination can better himself."

"At whose expense?"

"Don't ask silly questions," said O'Rourke. "What are you? A communist or something?"

They left the Rocket Tile office and, with O'Rourke in the lead, took the subway uptown twenty-eight blocks and shortly arrived at La Bete Noire, a chic bistro where they had been employed the previous year tiling the rest rooms.

"Do you remember this place?" said O'Rourke.

"Yes I do," said Maurice.

"You remember that we did a rather elaborate custom job on the shithouses. You also remember where they are, downstairs on the left. I want you to take this," O'Rourke produced a small cold chisel from his pocket, "and pull as many tiles off the wall as discretion allows."

"What!?" said Maurice.

"Please don't get excited," said O'Rourke. "The grout is probably stained and mildewed, a few tiles may be cracked already. It is time for a complete overhaul. Call it planned obsolescence, if you will."

"I don't believe you're saying this to me!" Maurice sputtered.

"Who else would I say it to?" said O'Rourke. "After a decent interval, I will present myself to the management, deplore this sort of senseless vandalism and offer our services of repair. I'm sure it's all covered by insurance anyway."

"You've got it all figured out, don't you?! Why do I have to be the one to do it?"

"Because my large presence would be noted," said O'Rourke. "You have a talent for fading into the woodwork. Don't think. Act." He slapped the cold chisel in Maurice's hand.

"Why don't we just get some guns and rob a bank?!" Maurice protested.

"It may come to that yet," O'Rourke replied. "Unfortunately our funds are not even sufficient to purchase a couple of Saturday night specials."

"I don't believe this," Maurice muttered.

"Go," O'Rourke commanded. "And may Allah be with you."

O'Rourke paced the sidewalk up the block for ten minutes until Maurice reappeared.

"The foul deed is done. Let's get out of here."

"Excellent!" O'Rourke exulted. "What are those bulges in your pockets?"

"Tiles," said Maurice. "I took all the ones that would be most difficult to replace."

"That's the spirit! We will celebrate with a six pack. Perhaps, the call from La Bete Noire will come sooner than we think."

O'Rourke and Maurice returned to the Rocket Tile office and whiled away the afternoon in idle storytelling, waiting for the call that never came.

"I don't understand this," said O'Rourke. "Certainly they must have noticed the damage by now. Would it be too unseemly to pay them a visit and point it out myself?"

Maurice took the question as rhetorical and did not bother to respond.

The next day, though, there was still no blinking red light on the answering machine and O'Rourke deemed that the time had come to drop by the scene of the crime. Maurice had taken the day off to attend to some errands so O'Rourke took the subway to the bistro in the mid-afternoon between lunch hour and dinner. He hoped to catch the management during a lull in business so that they might discuss the terms of the tile contract without interruption and it was his good fortune to find the owner at the bar doing some paperwork.

"Serge, how are you doing?" said O'Rourke. Serge was almost as fat as O'Rourke but shorter and softer. He looked up without recognition for a second, then he broke into a smile.

"Robair," he said. "Comment ca va?"

"Very well," said O'Rourke, "things couldn't be better. Busy, busy, busy."

Serge made with a Gallic shrug. "Work and money. I have so much of both I don't know what to do with them."

O'Rourke chuckled politely and Serge ordered the bartender: "Give Robair anything he wants."

"Thanks very much, Serge. I'll have a bourbon and water," said O'Rourke.

"So what brings you here?" said Serge. "I don't see you around much anymore."

"I've been trying to cut down on my drinking," O'Rourke lied brazenly. "Just a snort every now and again."

"Robair on the wagon," said Serge. "It sounds almost impossible. I remember when you guys were working here we had to lock up all the liquor."

"Ah, those carefree, sunlit days," said O'Rourke. "No more of that for me."

He was getting more and more uncomfortable. Why hadn't Serge mentioned the tile damage? Was it possible that no one had noticed it?

"Excuse me a moment," said he to Serge. "I must avail myself of the facilities." He went downstairs and entered the mens' room. Maurice had done a damn good job. Whole rows had been stripped from the walls and quite a few of the remaining tiles had been chipped or cracked. Even a substantial patch of the floor had been peeled up. There was no way the destruction could have gone unnoticed.

O'Rourke returned to the bar where Serge was still hunkered down over his paperwork. "What on earth happened to the mens' room?" he said, feigning stunned surprise. "It looks like someone threw a bomb in there."

"Isn't that something?" said Serge. "Some jerk must have gone nuts. Wrecked the whole place."

"Terrible thing," said O'Rourke. "You don't have any idea who did it?"

"I'm not sure but I think it was this drunk who comes in every few days. One time he pulled the pisser off the wall."

"Well, the damage is done," said O'Rourke

solemnly.

"Oh, yes, we must fix it immediately," said Serge.

"We're pretty booked up right now but, given the circumstances, we could make some time for you this week."

Serge looked puzzled. "Some time for what?" he said.

Is this a language problem? thought O'Rourke.

"Some time to repair the tile in the mens' room."

"Ohh," said Serge and laughed. "It's very kind of you to offer but we are going to try something else."

"Something else?" said O'Rourke. "You mean you're going to use another tile man?"

"Oh no, of course not," said Serge. "Let me show you."

He led O'Rourke to a storage room at the rear of the kitchen where there were five masonite panels leaning against the wall. Serge pulled the top one back and revealed that the hidden side was imprinted with a grid pattern that simulated a four and a quarter, tile wall in baby blue.

The revelation staggered O'Rourke. "Begab!" he said to himself. "It is the dread Barclay board!"

"My nephew is just going to cover the walls down there with this stuff," Serge explained. "That way we don't have to worry about vandalism anymore."

O'Rourke was aghast. "But this is a high class place," he sputtered. "You can't have bathrooms that look like a cheesy Chinese restaurant."

"Hey, my designer says that this stuff is very chic lately, tres retro," said Serge. "It doesn't cost shit either."

At that moment, O'Rourke would have strangled the entire French people if he could have just got his hands around their collective neck. Tres retro! And real cheap too!

He did a decent job of restraining himself, and, after going through all the appropriate departure rituals, O'Rourke hit the street in a very brown study indeed.

"The unmitigated gall!" he fumed. "The man is a complete philistine! We go to the trouble to create something elegant, something wonderful, and he replaces it with Barclay board!"

He was in such a state that he did not notice the body lying across the sidewalk until he tripped over it. He looked down and there was a toothless, old face grinning up at him.

"I am you and you are me," said the reclining figure, who was wrapped up in the filthiest ski parka that O'Rourke had ever seen. "How about a drink?"

He held up a quart of Colt 45.

"Had mine already," said O'Rourke. "Why are you lying across the sidewalk where innocent pedestrians like myself can stumble over you?"

"The sidewalk's where the heat is," said the old bum. "Just get down here and you can feel it."

"I'll take your word for it," said O'Rourke. "and I thank you for your kind offer."

"Hey, you buy, I buy, what's the difference? This town has been a party ever since I got here."

"The party's over," O'Rourke grumbled. "You're just the last one to leave."

"Leave? What are you, crazy? This is New York! The Big Apple! The top of the heap! If you can make it here, you can make it anywhere!"

O'Rourke was almost overwhelmed by an irrational impulse to crush the old bum's skull with a large stone but there was none lying around. Instead, he moved on down the street leaving the crazy fool to revel in the wonders of the metropolis.

By the time O'Rourke got back to the Rocket Tile office, Maurice had turned up with a couple of beers and a pint of Heaven Hill.

"It is good you have brought these things," said O'Rourke, "for they will cushion the blow."

"I guess we didn't get the job," Maurice correctly surmised.

"Not only do we not get the job but our original work is to be replaced with cheesy, fake tile paneling."

Maurice chuckled. "Hey, that's progress. Well, have a snort," he said and poured some whiskey into a paper cup.

"Don't mind if I do," said O'Rourke. "This reminds me of another incident where an acquaintance of mine set out to create his own employment. His name was Coriolanus Cheezowitz."

"That name has a familiar ring to it," said Maurice.

"I may have mentioned him on some previous occasion," said O'Rourke. "Stop me if the story begins to resemble a deja vu."

"Believe me, I will."

"I knew I could count on you, Maurice. Now, let me say from the beginning that Coriolanus Cheezowitz was the victim of a checkered career which had led him up more blind alleys than you've had hot dinners. The man, while brilliant in many ways, was a certifiable loser and a social pariah. His problems were too myriad for me to enumerate, but they were just about all poor Cheezowitz had. He was constantly in need of funds and would often turn his considerable, if twisted, intellect to the formation of get-rich-quick schemes.

"One day, while he was sitting in a trashy bar frequented by that echelon of Bowery bums who consider themselves a superior species to their street dwelling brethren because they receive a biweekly welfare check that allows them to slug down a shot and a beer somewhere other than the corner, Cheezowitz overheard a conversation about Central American insects. One of the old juiceheads, 'a charter member of the Explorer's Club', was railing on about these giant cockroaches from Costa Rica. 'Big as wolverines and twice as nasty!' Cheezowitz became curious and tried to ask a few questions, but the gentleman turned belligerent and rudely suggested that Cheezowitz take his questions and go fuck himself. Cheezowitz often had this effect on people.

"He was not, however, deterred by the rebuff, and even though he assumed the old rummy was exaggerating, launched his own investigation into the possible existence of such a fabulous creature."

"What was he?" said Maurice. "Some kind of bug freak?"

"Not at all," said O'Rourke. "He was one of those visionaries who can see the inherent opportunities in almost any situation. He repaired to the library and discovered that, indeed, there is a cockroach indigenous to the Central American rain forest called the Megablatta. It has several characteristics of no interest to anyone but an entomologist and is distinguished only by its unusual size. Some of these bugs grow to be a foot long."

"I'd like to see a few of those run for cover when the light goes on."

"Now you are thinking in a pure Cheezowitzian mode," said O'Rourke. "Coriolanus scrounged around for materials in those plastic supply places on Canal Street and built a giant version of the Combat roach trap. It was a foot high, two feet in diameter and had four large openings at the quadrants. Inside, he placed a cheesecake laced with insecticide."

"He was going to sell this thing to the Costa Ricans?"

"That was his claim," O'Rourke replied. "He arranged passage on a banana boat to the port of Limon and managed to stay in Costa Rica for several weeks before the authorities tracked him down and kicked him out. He came back in a white linen suit with extravagant, unlikely tales of all the deals he had made.

"Two weeks later, the real purpose of his mission began to surface in the tabloid press – reports of cockroaches the size of rats in Brooklyn, panicky confrontations in Manhattan kitchens, befuddled exterminators. Surely you remember all the uproar, Maurice – 'Invasion of the Colossal Bugs!', stuff like that."

"Can't say as I do."

"Before your time, perhaps. Throw me one of those beers." O'Rourke popped the top and continued. "Well, that's when Cheezowitz emerged from the shadows. He started advertising his giant roach trap on late night, cable TV. I can see him now, his newscaster wig and zoot suit haranguing the bleary viewers: 'So you say you're not getting enough for your money! You've tried everything but you're still not satisfied! Who would be with giant insects running around their kitchen?! It's time to do something about it! The "Bugger Off" cockroach killer is guaranteed to get fast results! But hurry! Supplies are limited!' Very limited, apparently. The orders rolled in but the traps did not roll out. Cheezowitz was boarding a plane to the Cayman Islands with a suitcase full of cash when the Feds bagged him with an indictment for mail fraud."

"You're losing me here," said Maurice. "Where did these giant cockroaches come from in the first place?"

"Haven't you been listening to me? They came

from Costa Rica," O'Rourke replied. "How they got here only Cheezowitz knows."

"What happened to them? I've never seen one around."

"They did not find apartment dwelling to their liking and descended into the sewers where they now live happily with the alligators." The telephone rang.

"Avast!" said O'Rourke. "Are we perhaps on the verge of doing some business?"

Maurice picked up the receiver. "Rocket Tile.... Could you hold on a second?" He put his hand over the mouthpiece. "There's some woman on the phone who claims you're her husband."

"Some woman who's not my ex-wife?"

"Definitely."

"Ask her how much money she has."

Maurice took his hand off the mouthpiece. "Listen, he just went out. If you could leave your name and number . . . hey, I'm sorry lady. I just work here." He hung up. "Testy old bitch!"

"Let me guess," said O'Rourke. "Alice Port."

"That's what she said."

"It must be a full moon."

"The name sounds familiar. Who is she?"

"That story is for another day," said O'Rourke.

"Let us secure the locks and be on our way. They are coming out of the woodwork, Maurice, and it is time to lay low."

They left the office and were almost immediately confronted on the street by a stolid old gentleman in a worn blue suit and grey felt hat. He peeled off a flyer from a stack under his arm and insistently handed it to O'Rourke. The printing was large and read:

The End is near! You have missed the Rapture and you are going to Hell! Your only chance of being saved is to GET YOUR HEAD CUT OFF!! (Rev. 20:4)

This advisory notice was accompanied by a rendering of the Devil standing in front of the Vatican flirting with a lascivious nun.

"Now wait a minute," said O'Rourke. "What does this mean?"

"It means exactly what it says," said the old man as solemnly as a judge pronouncing a death sentence.

"I can understand what it says," O'Rourke replied, " but exactly how does one go about getting his head cut off?"

"Any way you can," the old man answered.

"Perhaps you have some suggestions," said O'Rourke. "This is all new to me and I haven't given it much thought."

"I'll say you haven't," the old man scoffed. "That's why you missed the Rapture."

"Yes, I realize that, but what do I do now?" O'Rourke persisted.

The old man's demeanor changed. He was suddenly conspiratorial. "There is a certain Chinese restaurant around the corner, the Kar Ho. There is a man there who chops vegetables. His name is Sammy Wing and he will cut off your head with his cleaver if you give him ten dollars."

"Sammy Wing, huh? Gee, I don't know if I have ten dollars," said O'Rourke going through his pockets.

"You can haggle. The Chinese like to haggle. That is why they are called the Jews of the East."

"Well, listen, there's two of us, you know. I don't suppose we could touch you for a few bucks?"

The old man bristled. "Certainly not." He focused his flinty gaze on O'Rourke. "I believe you are having me on. I have given you the best advice you'll ever get and you mock me."

"Since when is being broke a sin?" O'Rourke countered. But don't worry. We will call Sammy Wing when we can afford him. Good day and God bless."

The old man did not take his hard eyes off O'Rourke and Maurice until they passed from his view around the corner. He then continued on his way, sidestepping two bums sprawled sleeping on the sidewalk. They were, after all, beyond salvation.

A COUNTRY SOJOURN 6

"Ah, for the life of a yard person of the African-American persuasion in the old Dominion!" master tile mason Robert O'Rourke exulted as he and his assistant Maurice crept along behind a slow moving pickup truck in their rented van. The tailgate of the pickup hung open and a black man in overalls and nothing else sat with his legs dangling from the rear staring sullenly at the traffic behind. The box he sat in was piled with manure and the aroma hung in the humid air like the notes of an advertising jingle; pungent, familiar, and mildly offensive.

"Just look at that poor devil."

"Watch your mouth," said Maurice, "we are deep in alien corn."

"Quite right," said O'Rourke. "I must take care not to identify myself with the rest of the cornpone cracker population hereabouts."

Hereabouts was the east shore of the Chesapeake Bay near the small town of Chatham. O'Rourke and Maurice had contracted to set tile in the kitchen of an estate outside the town and quit New York that very morning for the drive south.

"We are close, Maurice, very close. I can smell it."

"I'll say," Maurice agreed.

"So close to the end of our journey a powerful thirst has come upon me." The pickup truck turned off the road into a driveway and O'Rourke stepped on the gas.

"We shall stop at the first watering hole we come upon and stock up."

A half an hour later, after passing through town, stopping at the Seven Eleven for a case of beer, getting lost, turning around in front of the general store in the tiny hamlet of Boze Corner, retracing their route to the right turnoff, and driving through the fields of the estate, O'Rourke and Maurice arrived at the main house.

"Begab!" said O'Rourke, "these people have a few bucks I'd say."

Waiting to greet them was the general contractor who had a real name but was known to O'Rourke and Maurice as The Thork. To his face, the article was dropped as in, "Where's the money, Thork?" The Thork was married to a woman whose father had recently inherited this very estate from his late aunt and The Thork had been engaged to restore the decaying property.

O'Rourke got out of the van and stretched.

"Hello there, Thork!" he hailed. "I had no idea how much money you married. Rich women are a full time job though. I hope you're up to all the challenges that face you."

The Thork, who had once actually held a job sawing off the top of dead peoples' heads for autopsies, grinned lamely. He loved his wife. He loved her family's money. His good luck filled him with such a sense of potential loss that he required the twice-weekly services of a psychoanalyst and a prescription for pills to put him to sleep.

O'Rourke looked down the gently sloping lawn to a wooden boat dock jutting into this backwater of the bay. The end of the dock had been expanded by The Thork into a platform with benches, suitable for cocktails by the water.

"Quite a spread indeed."

"I have to drive back to New York tonight," said The Thork. "Let me show you the job."

"Leaving so soon?" said O'Rourke. "We shall certainly suffer from the lack of your supervision."

"Better you should suffer than enjoy yourselves. These people are my relatives so I don't want to see any funny stuff."

The Thork was referring to a practice that had

become customary with O'Rourke and Maurice to leave behind some objet constructed of the leftover materials from the job. For example, the last time they had worked for The Thork, Maurice had molded a cement tableau of a creature that looked like a cross between the Buddha and a voodoo doll having its way from the rear with a fetching female figure whose back was covered with streamers of white caulk. It was not an easy work to look upon with detachment and it was so heavy The Thork had been obliged to smash it to pieces with a sledgehammer to nullify its hideous and powerful presence lest the client identify the thing with his own, that is, The Thork's worthy self.

"What you refer to as 'funny stuff'," said O'Rourke, "we view as imaginative expression. Of course, I wouldn't expect a crass philistine such as yourself to have any appreciation for the higher values."

"None at all," said The Thork, "so don't waste any of your creative juices on the likes of me or my family."

"Such delicacy, Thork, such consideration to take into account the possible prejudices of your deep-pocketed mom and dad-in-law," said O'Rourke.

"Your selflessness is an inspiration to us all, I'm sure."

They entered the house through the front door and were immediately faced with a disproportionately wide staircase running from the foyer to the second floor.

"What was this place?" said O'Rourke. "A set for one of those gwine-up-to-heaven movies?"

The Thork ignored O'Rourke's question and conducted them through the dining room into the gutted kitchen. "As you can see," he said, "I've cleaned it out. All you have to do is set the floor."

"And so we shall, Thork. We will make a floor the likes of which the neighborhood has never seen."

"You will make a floor exactly according to the architect's specs," said the Thork. "I've got to get out of here so make yourselves at home. The place has seven bedrooms."

And so the Thork departed, leaving O'Rourke and Maurice sitting on the porch quaffing beer, wondering where to get something to eat.

"We shall drive into town and seek out an oyster house. The area is celebrated for the aphrodisiac quality of its bivalves," said O'Rourke. "I've been told that a dozen Chincoteagues will turn a meek country parson into a raving Priapic monster."

"That gives us quite a head start," said Maurice.

"We shall then investigate the fabled local night

life. I understand the good burghers of Washington D.C. think of Chatham as a sort of miniature Juarez, a town where you can really let your hair down."

"I've never heard that before," said Maurice.

"Of course you haven't. It's their dirty little secret."

And so O'Rourke and Maurice unloaded their tools from the van and drove into town.

"It certainly doesn't look like sin city to me," said Maurice as they tooled down the main drag, past a couple of gas stations, a Dairy Queen, a bait shop and a combination beer, cigarette and video rental emporium.

"We must dig deeper," said O'Rourke. "We will drive down to the shore where we shall certainly find a suitable waterfront dive for our purposes."

"What purposes are those?"

"How should I know?" said O'Rourke. "All will be revealed in good time."

There was nothing on the water but a large, practically empty marina adjoined by a two story building with a sign that read: CHATHAM YACHT CLUB.

"This must be the place," said O'Rourke. "Note how cleverly they have disguised this sinkhole of depravity as a place you might bring your own mother."

They parked the van and walked around to the entrance where a bronze plaque informed: MEMBERS ONLY.

"You see," said O'Rourke, "engorged members only".

"I don't know about you," said Maurice, "but I'm not a member, engorged or otherwise."

"Just follow me," said O'Rourke. "We shall be welcomed as the sporting gentlemen that we are."

To Maurice's surprise, the maitre d', a young man in a white, vaguely naval uniform, did indeed welcome them and conduct them to a table overlooking the bay.

"Perhaps we can just sign a chit and beat the tab," said O'Rourke as he settled into his chair. "What is the name of Thork's father-in-law?"

"No idea, but I wouldn't advise using it. He's probably a regular."

"If any question arose, I would loudly denounce the man as an imposter and have him blackballed. Imagine how grateful Thork's wife would be if her father was barred for life from this unsavory gin mill Speaking of which, I need a drink."

A young girl, attired in the same sort of nautical apparel as the maitre d', arrived to take their order.

"I would like a double Tennessee walking whiskey and a pitcher of rainwater," said O'Rourke. "What will you have, Maurice?"

"Wait a minute," said the waitress, who wore a plastic name card on her lapel that read: JUNE. "I don't think we have that brand behind the bar. Would y'all like a Jack Daniel's instead?"

"That would do admirably," said O'Rourke. "My associate would like a vodka martini on the rocks. He prefers Old Rasputin, but Catherine the Great will do."

"I'll see," said the waitress dubiously and headed off to the bar.

"We have arrived, Maurice. We must question this young vixen and find out where the action is."

"The action has packed up and left," said Maurice. "I think this must be the off-season."

"Sin knows no season," said O'Rourke. "It is here and we shall find it."

The waitress returned with their drinks in plastic cups. "Y'all ready to order now?"

"We are indeed," said O'Rourke. "Bring us two dozen of your finest oysters on the half shell."

"We don't serve 'em that way."

O'Rourke was taken aback. "You don't? How do you serve them?"

"Fried," said the waitress. "Or we can put them in the microwave for you."

"The microwave?!" O'Rourke was aghast.

"They're frozen. They come in a box. The microwave's the fastest."

"Do you mean to tell me that you don't have any fresh oysters on the premises?" said O'Rourke.

"We never do. They're slimy. Folks won't eat 'em."

"Folks, you say. Well, what sort of fresh fish do you have?" O'Rourke queried.

"We don't really have much of anything fresh in that line, sir. We've got fish and chips and fish sticks but they're frozen too."

O'Rourke looked pained. "I shall have a hamburger," he said. "Medium rare."

"I'll have the same," said Maurice.

The waitress left with their orders.

"Is this what it's come to, Maurice? Compressed fish paste processed on Japanese factory ships is the only seafood available on Chesapeake Bay? The future has overtaken us while we slept."

"There's nobody here," said Maurice. "No boats in the marina, no customers for the restaurant. We're lucky to get anything."

"A reasoned observation, Maurice. We have arrived at a lull in the busy life of Chatham," said O'Rourke sadly. "These forlorn and vacant boat slips do, however, strike some nostalgic nerve in my lower spine. Have I ever told you about my late Uncle Bug?"

"No, I don't believe you have," said Maurice.

"Excellent. I wouldn't want to bore you twice. Uncle Bug was a gentleman with a substantial independent income who went to all the right schools, knew all the right people, expressed all the right political opinions, wore all the right ties, in short – an insufferable boob. He was also a posh, society fag who loved to see his name in the gossip columns, fawned on movie stars and wealthy old widows, and made frequent visits to Tangier, Alexandria, Berlin – wherever the boys were willing and inexpensive. You know how the rich hate to spend money.

"Now, Bug had a close friend who had also gone to all the right schools and astoundingly emerged without a depraved bone in his body. He was called Stinky and he made his home in Old Woodbury, Long Island with a horsefaced wife and a neurasthenic, spinster daughter. He believed firmly that you should be mentioned in the newspaper only three times in your life; when you're born, when you get married, and when you get caught by the house dick with a hooker at the Plaza. No, just kidding. The man was a complete square. How he acquired his nickname I can only imagine.

"Uncle Bug and Stinky, so like and unalike in their ways, shared one passion – daysailing on Long Island Sound in Stinky's skiff with a canister of ice and a bottle of Scotch. Many was the afternoon they spent getting tanked as they tacked along the shore and reminisced about their school days. They waxed nostalgic about that world where the inferior races knew their place and gentlemen dressed for dinner. They mourned its passing."

The waitress returned from the kitchen with their hamburgers and set them down on the table. Each hamburger nestled on a plastic plate inside a circle of tiny plastic condiment containers.

"What is this?" said O'Rourke. "A dexterity test for monkeys? Are we unwitting participants in some sort of behavioral science experiment?"

"Beg pardon?" said the waitress.

"Please bring me another double," said O'Rourke. "It may act as a digestive aid by rendering me blind drunk so that I can't see what I'm eating. Now, where was I?"

"Out on the Sound with Bug and Stinky," Maurice prompted.

"Ah, yes, swilling Scotch on the bounding main. The sea is a fickle mistress, Maurice. One moment, she whispers sweet nothings while she nibbles your ear, the next, she's a raging harridan with blood in her eyes and murder in her soul. Uncle Bug and Stinky were sailing with the prevailing westerly breeze on a perfect, crystal clear afternoon when suddenly they found themselves surrounded by fog, caught in a cold clot of air that had blown in from the northeast and settled over the Sound. They could barely see a thing, but they were experienced sailors and set their course for the shoreline.

"Among the other small craft on the Sound that day was a cabin cruiser of the sort one sees berthed at the Montauk Yacht Club, a suburban living room on a floating platform with the cute name, 'Gone Shopping'. Marvin Kuntz, an oral surgeon from New Rochelle, and his wife Natalie were on their way back to their local marina when they were enveloped in the fog bank. Kuntz had never run into a situation like this before and, even though he had radar, sonar, and a Loran direction finder, he didn't know how to use any of them. Prior to that moment, piloting the 'Gone Shopping' had never required more skill than driving the car to the supermarket. Well, Marvin got very nervous and Natalie became almost hysterical. She'd always hated the boat anyway. She'd always known that something like this would happen. All they wanted was out of that pea soup fog and, in their panicked state, they were sure the only way to achieve that end was to let out the throttle and run for it.

"Imagine Bug and Stinky's surprise when the 'Gone Shopping' burst out of that Stygian mist like a bat out of Hell and bore straight down on them. Stinky tried to steer clear but the hog powerboat caught the skiff full in the side and tossed it right over. As the two old gentlemen floundered in the water, they could hear the sound of fiberglass being crushed as the overturned skiff's keel ripped a gash in the cabin cruiser's port side from its bow to its stern. Do you get the picture?"

"A real tragedy at sea in the making," said Maurice.

"Indeed it was. Bug and Stinky managed to pull themselves up on their overturned hull and watch the disabled cabin cruiser start to list badly to port as it took on water. Natalie Kuntz stood on the rear deck in high heels screeching for help. Her husband looked stunned at the water gushing around his feet. He hailed Bug and Stinky. 'We're sinking!'

" 'Damn tough luck!' said Uncle Bug, who was almost beside himself with anger. 'Shore's only a half mile or so! The swim should do you good!'

" 'Yes, the water's very invigorating this time of

year!' Stinky called out. 'You'll like it!'

"Well, that shut up Natalie in a hurry. The Kuntz's stared at Bug and Stinky in open-mouthed astonishment.

" 'What do you mean!?' said Marvin. 'You've got to let us come aboard your boat!'

" 'Wouldn't do at all,' said Bug. 'We have a problem with our rudder!'

" 'And we seem to have lost our sheet!' said Stinky. 'Not to mention our bottle of Scotch!'

" 'I've got a whole case of Scotch over here!' Marvin yelled back. 'See!' He waved two bottles in the air. 'Dewar's, of course,' Stinky muttered.

"Well, they probably would have gone on like that all day," said O'Rourke, "but natural forces suddenly intervened. With a great shudder, the 'Gone Shopping' listed sharply and threw the Kuntz's into the water. Within seconds, the thing sank like a rock.

" 'Now see here!' Bug loudly protested as the couple swam toward the capsized skiff. 'You are people we would never normally associate with, besides which, this is all your fault!'

" 'Law of the sea, old man,' said Stinky sadly. 'We are unfortunately obliged to take aboard any distressed person that comes our way.'

" 'A law that ought to be changed,' Bug said

indignantly as the Kuntz's clambered up on the other end of the hull. Natalie had not lost her spiked high heels in the disaster, which further infuriated Bug. 'What are you trying to do, woman?! Sink this one too?! Take off those shoes immediately!'

" 'Listen,' said Marvin, 'I don't think it's necessary to talk to my wife in that tone of voice. And they're very expensive shoes, by the way.'

"Stinky exploded. 'Do you mean to tell me that those shoes are worth more to you than than the hull of the craft which is presently preserving you from a watery grave?! By God, I'm a gentleman..!'

" 'I'll take off the shoes!' Natalie shrieked. 'They're ruined anyway!' As she removed her heels and tossed them in the water, she turned her wrath on her husband. 'This is all your fault! I hate boats! I always hated boats!'

" 'Then you ought to be happy!' Marvin spluttered back. 'Because it's gone! You can always get another pair of shoes!'

" 'Now see here,' said Bug impatiently, 'you have capsized our boat. You must help us right it.'

" 'I don't understand,' said Kuntz.

" 'Of course you don't,' Stinky snapped. 'That's why you have no business on the waterways. That's why you constitute a public menace!'

“ ‘I’m freezing,’ Natalie complained.

“Now just try to imagine, Maurice, the four of them, soaked to the skin, clinging to the keel of the overturned daysailer and bickering in the middle of a fog bank.”

“I’ve got the picture,” said Maurice. “It has a certain epic quality – the old men, the oral surgeon, the wife and the sea.”

“Yes, that’s it exactly,” said O’Rourke. “Cast adrift in the gloaming with no one but each other to cling to. So they thought at the time anyway. Uncle Bug and Stinky organized the first attempt to right the craft by moving the Kuntzes around to their side of the keel.

“ ‘We must lean back with all our weight and pull the boat over,’ said Stinky.

“ ‘Are you crazy?!’ Natalie wailed. ‘We’ll all go in the water!’

“ ‘That is correct,’ said Stinky.

“ ‘I won’t do it!’ said Natalie.

“ ‘You will do as you are told,’ said Stinky. ‘If you wish to impede our efforts, I suggest you find another hull to stand on.’

“After some more discussion, Marvin induced his wife to cooperate by promising to never go to sea again if they ever got back to dry land. They all four leaned back and the keel tilted with them. Their combined weight was not quite sufficient, however, to overturn the boat, though the mast actually appeared briefly on the surface before the keel snapped back to an upright position leaving all save Marvin in the water. The oral surgeon hung on resolutely and was catapulted twenty feet through the air into the water on the other side of the capsized craft.

"It took a few minutes for all of them to struggle back up onto the hull where Mrs. Kuntz gave Bug and Stinky a piece of her mind. 'Any more bright ideas?' she snarled. 'Maybe we should just drown ourselves now and get it over with!'

" 'Please feel free to do so,' Bug replied. 'I, for one, shall do nothing to stop you.'

" 'Now, listen here,' Marvin gasped with streamers of snot and seawater hanging from his nose. 'You've got to stop being rude to my wife...'

"And that's when they heard it, Maurice, the distant putter of an outboard motor moving slowly in their direction. For a short moment they were silent, as if they couldn't believe their ears. Then they all started yelling at once as a small cigarette boat emerged from the fog. The speedboat did not respond. In fact, it veered away and shut off its engine about fifty feet off their starboard.

" 'Ahoy!' Stinky called out. 'We need help!'

"There was no response from the speedboat but the sound of two men arguing in Spanish carried across the water.

" 'Now what's going on here,' said Bug indignantly. 'They are ignoring us.'

" 'Don't leave us here!' Natalie screeched.

"The continuing argument in Spanish wafted through the fog.

" 'This is the damnedest rude behavior . . .' Stinky muttered just as the speedboat started up again and nosed around. It slowly cruised in their direction and came to a stop about fifteen feet away. Two swarthy men, one of them with a mustache, peered from the cockpit at our four castaways on the hull.

" 'What's the problem?' said the clean-shaven one with a heavy Hispanic accent.

" 'What's the problem?!' Stinky declaimed in exasperation. 'The problem is obvious! We have capsized and we need your help.'

" 'What do you want us to do about it?' said the man in the speedboat.

" 'Get us off this thing and take us to shore!' Natalie howled.

" 'You can't come on this boat,' said the swarthy man.

" 'Why not?!'

" 'Because I said so,' he replied flatly.

" 'Now wait a minute!' said Marvin.

" 'The man is certainly exhibiting more sense than we did,' said Bug to Stinky.

" 'We don't want to come aboard your boat,' said Stinky. 'We just need a tow close enough to shore to right ourselves without half drowning.'

"The two men spoke in Spanish. 'Okay,' said the clean-shaven one, 'we'll throw you a line.'

"Which they did. In due time, Bug and Stinky secured the line to the keel, signaled to the men in the speedboat and off they went, heading for the North Shore. In a matter of minutes, they passed out of the fog into bright sunlight. The shoreline was no more than a quarter mile away. Stinky called out to the men in the speedboat not to go any further. The Sound is very shallow in that area and he was worried that the mast would hit the bottom and snap off. His point, however, was rendered moot by the appearance of two Coast Guard boats bearing down on them at high speed from the east. The two swarthy men started yelling at each other and the one with the mustache brandished a machete. He cut the line to the sailboat keel and the cigarette boat sped off toward New York. One of the Coast Guard boats gave chase, the other pulled alongside the capsized sailboat. A fifty caliber machine gun and numerous automatic rifles were trained on our bedraggled foursome."

Maurice broke into laughter. "Did they catch the cigarette boat?"

"I have no idea. God, is this hamburger terrible or what?"

"Pretty bad. What happened after that?"

"Bug and Stinky and the Kuntzes were all placed under arrest and thrown in the brig in manacles. After several hours of interrogation on shore, they were all released. Uncle Bug contracted pneumonia and passed away a week and a half later. The society word-of-mouth had it that he died of AIDS but Stinky knew better. He renamed his sailboat, "Bug". I don't know what happened to the Kuntzes or the Colombian good Samaritans."

"A tragic ending," said Maurice.

"To a tragic meal," said O'Rourke as the busboy approached their table. They watched in silence as he pushed everything on the table – plastic cups, plastic plates, plastic forks, plastic squeeze bags – into a plastic garbage bag in a plastic garbage can that he had dragged over.

"Some opt for elegance, others for progress," said O'Rourke philosophically. "I opt for settling the bill and getting out of here. We shall search out another dive for a nightcap."

7
A COUNTRY SOJOURN CONTINUED

Master tile mason Robert O'Rourke awoke and found himself in a four poster bed with sunlight streaming through the open window that afforded him a squinting view of two horses grazing in the distance. He was not accustomed to these pastoral circumstances and, for a moment, did not realize where he was. His recollections were fragmentary and only slowly came together like the pieces of a jigsaw puzzle. He lay in bed until the picture began to take form.

"I am in Maryland in the country house which the Thork's in-laws inherited from their late aunt," he said to himself. "I am here to tile the kitchen floor." It was not a pleasant prospect, but then, tiling kitchen floors never was.

"What have I done to myself?" he groaned as he recalled the previous evening with dull horror. "I am lucky to be alive. Or not so lucky at that."

He and his assistant Maurice had arrived back at

the house after dining in the insufferably dull town of Chatham and discovered a box in the living room with a collection of miniature liqueur bottles – creme de menthe, Fra Angelica, triple sec, you name it. Greatly inspired by the little colored bottles, which in his whiskatory state shimmered like jewels, O'Rourke had organized a game of chess a la Our Man In Havana. Each bottle was a piece and each piece taken was consumed by its captor. O'Rourke could not remember who had won or if anyone had won at all. He could not remember how he had gotten into this four poster bed. But there he was with an onerous tile job staring him right down the throat.

"I cannot do it," he moaned. "I will sneak downstairs out of this house and run away to Mexico. They will never catch me there."

He rolled out of the bed and found his pants on the floor. He pulled them on and decided to find the bathroom. His first attempt to leave the unfamiliar room was a failure; the door he tried opened into an empty closet that smelled of mildew and naptha. It filled him with an overwhelming sense of desolation.

"What did I do in my past life to deserve this?" he asked himself. "Whatever it was, it must have been bad."

He tried the next door with more luck. It led to the hallway. He padded along, opened the first door he came to, and found Maurice snoring away, sprawled on a mattress on the floor.

"Let him sleep," thought O'Rourke. "No nightmare could be as bad as what he will soon wake to."

He closed the door gently and proceeded down the hall until he found a bathroom. His own reflection in the mirror over the sink gave him quite a start. His gray-green face was mottled with flaring red blotches and looked like nothing so much as a photograph he'd seen of the surface of one of Jupiter's moons.

"I am dead," he concluded. "Nothing living could possibly look like this."

As he stared at this hideous apparition that was himself, another appalling set of memories burbled up from the black pit in his skull. He recalled that he and Maurice had not come straight back to this place from the Chatham Yacht Club. They had stopped at a roadhouse and ordered cocktails at the bar. The only other patrons were a couple – an overweight, gum chewing, bleached blonde in tight black pants and her male friend, a lanky, hostile looking individual sporting a baseball cap. They were having an argument that quickly erupted into a shouting match. The bartender paid no attention whatever to their public display of disaffection. The blonde abandoned her mate, huffed over to the bar and plopped herself down right next to O'Rourke.

"You guys look kind of interesting," she'd purred. "Y'all must be from out of town because there's sure no one interesting around here."

One nervous glance confirmed to O'Rourke that the boyfriend was glowering at his back and clenching an empty beer bottle tight enough to make his knuckles turn white.

"Well, we are from out of town," O'Rourke allowed, "but we're not really very interesting." That's when he felt the hand close on his shoulder.

"Y'all trying to make time with my girl just cuz she's drunk as shit?" the fellow in the baseball cap growled. The bartender stood well away with a sly smile on his face.

"No . . . ," said O'Rourke.

"Well, why not? You blind or something? Ain't she pretty enough for you? Or maybe you're one of these Yankee sissies. One thing I hate is Yankee sissies."

It was a tiresome old routine that O'Rourke had heard in so many different versions that the initial distaste he felt for this lout and his porcine moll was for sheer lack of originality. He was by no means a barroom brawler, but the situation seemed to call for an immediate preemptive strike.

"If I've offended you in any way..." he began as he grabbed the man's other arm, which he correctly surmised was the one attached to the beer bottle, whirled around with surprising agility for a man of his age and girth, and threw his drink in the lout's face. Things happened very quickly after that. Following a clumsy flurry of blows, the lout lay on the floor with both O'Rourke and Maurice kicking him. The girlfriend was caterwauling hysterically - "You leave my LeeRay alone!"- and the bartender had pulled a length of pipe from under the counter which he brandished at them with unfriendly intent.

"Get the fuck outta here!!" he yelled.

Maurice and O'Rourke backed out the door – "Thank you so much for this demonstration of Southern hospitality," said O'Rourke. "Give us a call if there are any good lynchings coming up" – and they raced for their parked van, started up and took off, leaving the bartender standing silhouetted in the doorway waving his pipe and yelling insults at them.

This was the episode that O'Rourke remembered as he studied his ravaged face in the bathroom mirror. The implications were terrible. Word of the incident would spread through the tobacco road environs of Chatham like an epidemic and the enraged locals would swarm down on the Yankee city slickers with pitchforks and rope and flaming hickory sticks. Was this to be O'Rourke's last stand – slaughtered in the boonies by a howling mob of yahoos? It was too much to bear. But wait! A glimmer of hope was already shining through the gathering black clouds in O'Rourke's fevered brain. No one knew their purpose in Chatham. No one knew they were there. All they had to do was stay inside and not leave the estate until the job was completed. Then they could make a run for it in the wee hours of the morning. But preparations must be made for the siege. They had no supplies. A lightning raid on the general store at Boze Corner was the only solution. Beans and beer would see them through.

O'Rourke lurched back down the corridor to the room where Maurice was sleeping.

"Wake up!" he shouted. "The barbarians are at the gate!"

Maurice looked up in bleary alarm at the crazy man gesticulating over him.

"There is not a moment to lose! Everything depends on immediate decisive action!"

"Go away," said Maurice. "Leave me and my bad

head alone."

"You won't have any head at all if you don't do as I say!" O'Rourke rebuked him ferociously.

"What the hell are you jabbering about?" Maurice was thoroughly annoyed.

"Think!" O'Rourke bellowed. "Surely you remember the disastrous events of last night!" He quickly recapitulated his analysis of their predicament.

"First you make me irritated, then you make me paranoid," Maurice grumbled as O'Rourke concluded his harangue. "If you're right, we are fucked."

"The dim bulb shines!" O'Rourke snorted. "We must load up at that general store immediately. It may be too late already. Perhaps we could put on good old boy drawls for their benefit."

"I don't think that will wash," said Maurice.

They hurried out to the van and drove off along the estate road to the entrance.

"We must make sure we are not followed," said O'Rourke. "When we leave the store I will drive like a madman."

Maurice shot O'Rourke an alarmed sideways glance but said nothing as they sped down the pitted two-lane road toward Boze Corner.

The general store had an antique gas pump outside and a screened veranda that ringed three sides of the building. It looked like it might have once housed a restaurant where the gentry from the surrounding estates could drop in for a country dinner. What gentry was left went to Chatham now and the Boze Corner general store sat almost derelict by the side of the road like a bum sitting on an old car seat in a vacant lot.

O'Rourke slowed down well before their arrival to reconnoiter the situation from a distance. There was a lone pick-up truck parked out by the gas pump.

"With our luck, it will be LeeRay stopped in to chew a plug and whittle voodoo dolls by the cracker barrel," O'Rourke muttered.

He stopped a little past the store and backed in so as to be pointed in the right direction for a quick getaway.

"Say as little as possible. We should pretend we are deaf and speak in sign language."

"I don't think we want to attract any more attention than we have to," said Maurice impatiently.

"Only kidding," said O'Rourke. "You certainly can be testy in the morning."

They got out of the van and walked into the store. There was nobody there but an old man reading a newspaper behind the counter. He looked up at them and said: "Good morning."

O'Rourke returned the greeting with a little wave and a smile. Then he and Maurice proceeded to pillage the small canned goods section of the store. They took everything – red beans, black-eyed peas, okra, cut green beans, creamed corn, chili, Spam, Vienna sausage. The cans had been on the shelf long enough to collect a thick layer of dust. Then they scooped up several boxes of Ritz crackers and saltines and set everything down in front of the storekeeper who looked up from his Washington Post in astonishment. O'Rourke removed every stick of beef jerky from a jar on the counter while Maurice fetched three cases of beer from the cooler.

"Having a party?" said the man behind the counter.

"That's right, a party," said O'Rourke. "How much will all this be?"

"Well, let's see. What have you got there?"

It took him a torturously long time to add up all the items before he arrived at the figure of $87.49. O'Rourke peeled off five twenties from the eight hundred dollar wad he had in his pocket.

"You guys rob a bank or something?"

"That's right," said O'Rourke. "I'm Bonnie and this is Clyde."

The storekeeper chuckled. "Pleased to meet you. Have a nice day now," he said as they scuttled out the door with their hoard. They loaded the van and, after O'Rourke was convinced that no one was pursuing them, drove straight back to the estate.

"We are now prepared for any eventuality including nuclear war," he said as they turned down the road to the house. They unloaded everything into the empty living room but the beer. That they hung by strings off the dock to keep it cool.

"What now?" said Maurice.

"Loathsome as it sounds, we have to do this fucking tile job," said O'Rourke.

And do it they did. Maurice mixed cement all day as O'Rourke lay down a slab to level the kitchen floor. The discrepancy between the north and south walls was more than three inches. By the end of the day, they had poured so much concrete, O'Rourke remarked that it was like parking a loaded dumptruck in the house.

"We can only hope to have disappeared when the whole thing collapses into the basement. Perhaps the Thork will garner a substantial inheritance sooner than he thinks."

"Perhaps he planned it this way and we're the fall

guys," Maurice suggested.

"The Thork? I wouldn't give him credit for that much imagination, but you never know. We shall leave something behind to protect the slab from evil spirits."

"There is enough mud left over for the purpose," said Maurice.

They commenced work on the totem immediately. O'Rourke packed a pair of rubber gloves with wet concrete while Maurice wired up a form for the torso of the thing and covered it with a thin layer of cement. They left these parts to dry on a piece of plywood in the driveway and adjourned to the veranda for a tall, cool one.

"We are going through our beer supply at an alarming rate," said O'Rourke. "We must conduct a thorough search of the house. It has already yielded up that horrible liqueur collection and may contain other caches of intoxicating beverages. I suggest we begin in the cellar. It is the sort of place where on old lady might stash a few bottles of sherry."

The stone cellar walls were covered with long, caked streaks where salt water was seeping in from the bay. The whole place smelled of brine and decay, rather like a sweaty armpit.

"We don't need any booze," said Maurice. "I'm getting pickled just standing here."

O'Rourke dug through a pile of boxes along the

wall but there was nothing in them but sodden old rags that might once have been table linen.

"Phew! This is some stinky shit!" he grimaced.

Further down the wall, daylight shone through a grate near the ceiling. Beneath this grate was a stack of wooden boxes. O'Rourke picked up the one on top and tried to pull off the cover.

"This is on here tight. I need a pry bar or something."

They took the box back upstairs to the pantry off the kitchen and found the appropriate tool for the job. The cover gave way with the screech that rusty nails make and revealed three dusty bottles packed in filthy old straw.

"Eureka," O'Rourke growled as he held one of the bottles up to the light. "Chateau Laffite, 1903. Gadzooks, we have stumbled on a treasure trove! Enough to send a dedicated oenophile into convulsions! Find me a corkscrew."

"I don't know," said Maurice dubiously. "What are the Thork's in-laws going to say when they find out we drank up the wine they planned to auction off at Sotheby's?"

"Wine is made to be enjoyed, not collected by a bunch of anal-retentive squares who wouldn't know who Bacchus was if he threw up on the dinner table and tried to make time with their teenage daughter," said O'Rourke. "The very act of leaving the stuff lying around since 1903 fills me with indignation. It is time to let this wine breathe!"

With that, O'Rourke took Maurice's Swiss army knife and pulled the cork. There was a hissing sound as a luminous cloud of white gas escaped from the bottle and hung in the air over their heads.

"Begab!" said O'Rourke, "I hope it hasn't turned."

The gas had a sharp, musky smell which lingered as the cloud slowly dissipated. O'Rourke held the bottle up to his nose. "What bouquet! A vintage year if there ever was one. Do we have any glasses?"

"There are only paper cups," said Maurice, "and I'm not sure I'd drink that stuff if I were you."

"You must be joking," said O'Rourke. "This may be the only opportunity you ever have to imbibe such a costly infusion of the grape." O'Rourke poured a cup and offered it to Maurice.

"You drink it," said Maurice. "If you don't fall over foaming at the mouth I'll give it a try."

"Here's mud in your eye," said O'Rourke and drank the wine. He smacked his lips and exclaimed:

"Delicious by any standard! Even one as low as mine. You must try it. Pure ambrosia." He poured another cup and handed it to Maurice who took a dubious sip. "What did I tell you?!" said O'Rourke. "Drink and be merry for tomorrow we tile!"

Maurice had to admit the wine was quite extraordinary as O'Rourke refilled his cup to the brim.

"Good enough for peasants like us. It shall see us through these troubled times."

They opened two cans of black-eyed peas and heated them on a small wood fire they built in the gravel of the driveway. This they accompanied with a jar of pickled beets and deviled ham spread on crackers.

"My cup runneth dry," said O'Rourke as he poured the last few drops from the bottle. "Would you do the honors, Maurice?"

Maurice left O'Rourke on the veranda and went into the house to fetch more wine. The musky odor from the first bottle had not diminished and seemed to have entrenched itself in the pantry. Maurice opened a window to air the place out and took a dusty bottle from the wooden crate. He pulled the cork and another cloud of white gas hissed out the neck. In the gathering dusk, the vapor glowed as if it were electrified. Its sharp smell was overwhelming in those close quarters and Maurice hastened back out the front door to the veranda.

"Did I ever tell you about the time I met the Dalai Lama?" said O'Rourke as Maurice poured him a cup from the newly opened bottle. "He was surrounded by fawning acolytes of the well-to-do, Occidental persuasion seeking to have their own elevated position in the social order confirmed as cosmologically ordained. Sort of John Calvin meets Fu Manchu. These simpering brown-nosers who prostrated themselves at the great Lama's feet or sat cross-legged before him with lunatic grins that I believe were meant to convey beatitude were however of no interest to me. What caught my attention were the Dalai Lama's extraordinary shoes. Sticking out from beneath his robes were two wing-tip brogans of the finest English manufacture."

"You're sure there were only two?" Maurice queried.

"An interesting question, Maurice," replied O'Rourke. "In the interests of accuracy I should say that I only saw two. If there were more, the esteemed religious leader did an exemplary job of hiding them. But to continue, the Dalai Lama made a little speech to the gathering, soliciting funds for the Tibetan guerrillas who were fighting to reinstall his own royal ass on the throne and blessed the assembly for their generosity. He passed close to me as he headed for the door and I couldn't resist asking him about his shoes. He became very animated and described in detail how they were custom made in London by a very prestigious firm. He offered me the address and told me to use his name if I wanted to order a pair."

"I can see it now," said Maurice, "Just tell them the Dalai Lama sent me."

"I thanked him and asked him if he might answer a personal question. 'All questions are personal,' said he. 'Fire away.' What I wanted to know was how he reconciled wearing the skin of a slaughtered animal with his Buddhist faith. He replied that whereas he would never kill a cow himself, what was the point of letting the skin go to waste if someone else did? I was piqued by the hypocrisy of this statement and asked him if he thought it was okay to be a cannibal if you didn't personally murder your meal. 'I am a strict vegetarian,' he replied, 'but I see no harm in making use of what is available.' With that, he whipped out the top of a human skull from under his robe and said, 'This is the head of a woman raped and murdered by Chinese soldiers. I use it to take my tea.'

Maurice howled. "I knew you were making this up."

"As Allah is my mistress, I mean, witness," said O'Rourke, "I confess to a certain amount of poetic license. I also notice that my cup runneth dry and cannot be replenished by the empty vessel before me. If you will be so kind as to lend me your corkscrew, I will open another bottle. I only hope this stuff is going to your head the way it's going to mine."

O'Rourke crab-walked into the house and made his way to the pantry. The musty, white cloud had not only failed to disperse, it seemed to have become more concentrated. It hung in the air about four feet above the floor as if it were the icing on an invisible layer cake. From this vapor came a voice. "Robert!"

In his pleasantly toasted state, O'Rourke was more curious than startled. "I know that voice," he said out loud.

"I should hope so," came the tart reply. O'Rourke peered into the cloud and tried to focus. There appeared to be a disembodied, translucent head floating in the densest concentration of the vapor.

"Mom," said O'Rourke in surprise, "what are you doing here? You're dead."

"Only stewing in my own juices, Robert," said

the head. "I am here to inform you of the error of your ways."

"I see," said O'Rourke. "How very original of you."

"You always were a smart aleck, Robert. You take after your father's side of the family."

"Certainly not yours, Mom. You don't have an ironic bone in your body."

"As you can see, I don't have any bones in my body," the head replied.

O'Rourke was not so far gone that he was willing to accept this vision at face value. He reminded himself that he was not required to speak with his own hallucinations.

"You're right about that," said the head, apparently reading his thought, "but you still have to listen."

"What are you doing here anyway?" O'Rourke complained. "You appear to be a by-product of fermentation. How did you get in that bottle? It was corked in 1903."

"Material barriers mean nothing to me. You were destined to open that wine, Robert," said the head. "That's why I chose it as a lodging. As you know, I don't approve of liquid spirits in any form so it hasn't been easy for me."

"I can imagine. So here I am and there you are," said O'Rourke. "What is it you have on your mind?"

"I am here to warn you that you are in great danger, you and your assistant Maurice," said the head. "There is another spirit that inhabits this house, a malevolent woman about my own age. She intends to do you harm."

"Thanks for the glad tidings," said O'Rourke. "Now, if it's alright with you..." He picked up the third bottle of wine and peeled off the foil cap. This illusion of his mother was beginning to annoy him. What on earth was going on in his besotted brain to conjure her up anyway?

"You know I don't approve of drinking," said the head sternly.

"Oh yes, I'm well aware of that," said O'Rourke as he pulled the cork from the bottle and another rush of gas hissed out into the air. "I wonder who's in this one?"

"You'll come to a bad end, Robert, mark my words," said the head. "I'd wash my hands of you if I had any."

"Just don't be here when I get back," said O'Rourke. "It's been a rough enough day already."

He lurched out of the house back out onto the

veranda and held up the wine bottle. "I'm being pursued by ghosts, Maurice, all that burdensome baggage we carry around called memory."

"Who were you talking to in there?" Maurice wanted to know.

"Nobody. My mother," said O'Rourke.

"Your what?"

"Just kidding, Maurice. I was practicing a fantasy speech to the joint session of the House and Senate. I'd tell those greaseballs a thing or two."

"I'm sure you would," Maurice agreed. "How about a refill?"

"You know, Maurice," said O'Rourke as he poured wine into Maurice's cup, "the trouble with this house is the very earth it sits on, a damp, spongy bog that absorbs everything above and distributes it by capillary action throughout the entire peninsula."

"I'm not sure I understand what you're getting at," said Maurice. "Is this a structural problem you're talking about?"

"That's certainly one way to put it," O'Rourke replied. "What I'm talking about is the poisonous nature of the history of this place. Every sorry thing that's ever happened in this sodden land is trapped, suspended in an emulsion right beneath our feet. They can talk about chemical residues and toxic waste until they turn blue in the face but this land has been despoiled forever by its own memories... slavery ... treachery... murder... It leeches across the countryside in alluvial plumes of despair. It hides in the ground and emerges in the drinking water, in the oyster beds, and the LeeRays. It surfaces under the light of the full moon which it is our privilege to be viewing at this very moment."

Maurice looked out over the water into the reflected moonlight and felt a small pop! in the back of his head. "I'm drunk," he said. "and we've got a long day tomorrow. I'm going to hit the sack." He left O'Rourke alone on the veranda to finish the wine and made his way upstairs to bed.

"Pleasant dreams," O'Rourke called after him and turned his attention back to the inlet. He was enjoying the play of moonlight on the rippling water around the dock when he suddenly got a start. There was something down there, something that moved quickly out of sight under the ramp.

"Jesus," O'Rourke muttered, "they are launching an amphibious assault on the place." He picked up the first thing at hand which was the half-empty bottle. He swilled off the contents in one great swig, then smashed the bottle on the veranda railing. He was left holding the neck with a vicious, jagged edge on the business end.

"I'm coming for you, LeeRay!" he bellowed, brandishing his weapon. He descended from the veranda with jerky, spastic determination, bobbing and weaving across the lawn toward the dock. "You can't run and you can't hide!" he roared.

"What the hell are you doing?!" Maurice called out from an upstairs window. "Have you gone nuts?!"

O'Rourke ignored the question and continued his erratic advance on the dock ramp. "Come out of there!" he bawled. "I kicked your hick ass once and I'll do it again!"

A clenched set of yellow teeth caught the light from the house, followed by the glitter of eyes behind a mask. A figure leapt from under the ramp and confronted O'Rourke face to face.

"You sonuvabitch!" O'Rourke snarled. "I'll show you who's a fucking Yankee sissy!"

The big boar raccoon with an oyster shell clutched in one paw stood up on his hind legs and snarled right back. O'Rourke was momentarily confused. "Don't fuck with my head, LeeRay!"

"Why are you calling that raccoon LeeRay?!" Maurice demanded from his vantage point on the second floor.

"People give animals names," said O'Rourke. "It's our nature."

"Go to sleep," said Maurice, "and leave that raccoon alone. He looks pretty nasty."

O'Rourke took this good advice and retreated back up the lawn as the raccoon disappeared into the night. He misstepped and found himself sprawled out in the grass. It did not seem worth the effort to go any further.

He was on low ground in a wide valley. The sun was shining, the birds were singing, the wildflowers were in bloom. But there was something else happening out on the horizon, there was something moving rapidly toward him, something vast and inexorable that stretched across the breadth of the valley. He stood and watched until he could make out its churning, frothing contour. It was a surging wall of water, a fifty-foot tidal wave crested with towering geysers of white spume. He had to get out of there, he had to reach high ground. He started running toward the hills that framed the valley. Now he could hear the distant roar of the wave as it bore down upon him. He would never make it. He already had a stitch in his side. He grabbed on to the trunk of a tree and held on for dear life as the wave crashed over him. The roots of the tree gave way and he was awash in the torrent. He couldn't breathe, he was going under...

"Wake up!" a voice called from far, far away. He opened his eyes. The sun was shining, the birds were singing and Maurice loomed over him like an angry god. "What the hell are you doing out here? I thought you'd keeled over for good."

"Sleeping al fresco," said O'Rourke, "a balm for the body and soul."

"We've got a floor to set," said Maurice.

"So we have," said O'Rourke, raising himself up on one elbow, "and a delicious prospect it is. There might perhaps be a beer lying around?"

"I'll get you one," said Maurice and headed down to the dock where the six-packs were hanging in the water.

O'Rourke stood up and examined the green stain that ran from the cuff of his jeans to the shoulder of his shirt.

Maurice returned with a dripping can and handed it over. "You're sure you need this? You're covered with enough chlorophyll to photosynthesize your own alcohol."

"This accursed place is not only turning me green, it's beginning to addle my pate," said O'Rourke. "We must finish up this job and get out of here as soon as possible."

They worked feverishly that day and knocked out the entire kitchen floor as the weather turned from bright sunlight to overcast gray. They would have to wait several hours to grout it so they set to work in earnest on the totem. "The evil spirits that inhabit this place shall not defeat us if we take proper care to protect ourselves," said O'Rourke as he stripped off the rubber glove molds from the pair of cement hands. "We must make something so hideous that nothing living or dead will want anything to do with us." They added a concrete, horned head to the prone torso and stuck half a beer can in as a snout. They attached the molded hands so that they looked as if they were reaching out to grab the viewer in an obscene embrace. They added stubby legs with cloven hooves. "We will let it dry and ponder a suitable place to leave it," said O'Rourke. "I feel more secure already. Now, why don't you haul up another case from the cellar, Maurice, while I prepare our dinner."

O'Rourke started a fire in the gravel and opened two cans of Dinty Moore beef stew. The cloud cover overhead was shading towards black and a stiff breeze was kicking up from the south. He saw a flash of light on the horizon but heard no thunder.

Maurice carried up another wooden case from the cellar to the pantry and pried off the top. He removed a dusty bottle and started to pull the cork but the pressure inside was so great that it blew the corkscrew right out of his hand. There was an explosive hiss and he found himself enveloped in a miasma of musty gas.

"Maurice," a voice called out.

He looked around and there was a woman floating just above the floor, a naked, young woman with large, firm breasts. She seemed very close and very far away at the same time.

"Don't you remember me, Maurice?" she said.

Maurice was flabbergasted. "Ellen, but..."

"I know, I was killed in a car crash. Everybody crashes sometime. Do you remember what we used to do in cars?"

"Well, yeah, sure... "

"You're blushing, Maurice. You were always so shy. But you really loved my tits, didn't you?" She cupped her hands under her breasts and looked down at them fondly. "I think you only liked me for my tits."

"I was just a kid," Maurice protested. "Tits meant a lot to me then."

"They still mean a lot to me." said O'Rourke as

he walked into the room. "What are you doing standing there talking to yourself with that bottle in your hand? I need a drink."

"Who's this?" said Ellen.

"Uh, this is Robert O'Rourke. We work together."

"Have you taken leave of your senses?" said O'Rourke. "Why are you introducing me to myself and giving me your resume?"

"Can't you see her?" said Maurice. "Over there."

"See who?"

Ellen laughed.

"You don't see a naked woman?" said Maurice.

"That's what you see? Sounds better than what I saw. Maybe I better leave you two alone."

"Don't pay any attention to him," said Ellen. "I have something to tell you."

"I'll just take that bottle," said O'Rourke, removing it from Maurice's hand. "There's a storm blowing in, so come get it while it's hot." He left the pantry and returned to his fire in the driveway.

"You must leave this house as soon as possible," said Ellen. "There are things here that you don't want to know about."

"You're telling me," Maurice agreed.

"This is no time to joke," said Ellen. "You must

leave here tonight. Now go tell your friend what I have told you."

"Hey, hold on there a minute..." said Maurice as Ellen dissolved back into the fog. In a matter of seconds, she was gone.

"Don't tell me," said O'Rourke when Maurice rejoined him outside. "Someone you know appeared in those wine fumes and gave you a hard time." A bolt of lightning arced across the southern sky.

"Someone I knew. Ellen Beckett. She's dead."

"Yes, of course," said O'Rourke, "but what did she have to say?"

"She told me we had to get out of here as soon as possible."

"I heard something similar last night," said O'Rourke as the rumble of distant thunder set the air tingling, "and that is exactly what we're going to do after we grout the kitchen floor. There is no use pushing our luck even if these ominous warnings do come from peculiar figments of our own imaginations. Besides, this place is getting on my nerves. Have some beef stew and pour yourself a cup of wine." A raindrop hissed in the fire. "Then let us move to the porch and watch the fireworks from there," said O'Rourke.

In a matter of minutes, lightning was flashing,

thunder was cracking, and the rain came pouring down in a warm, sticky torrent.

"I have never subscribed to the notion of life after death," waxed O'Rourke, "but there are, perhaps, residual pockets of neurotic energy that hang about after our earthly departure to nag and harass the living. Call them what you will – ghosts, bad vibes, paranoid delusions – but we are their victims and it falls on us to do battle with them."

"It falls on us to get our ass out of here," said Maurice. "I am not in a combative mood."

"We may have no choice in the matter. I fear the angry boil is coming to a head faster than we know. Let us grout that floor and be finished with our obligation to this melancholy place." They immediately adjourned to the kitchen and set to work at a frantic pace. An hour later, the storm outside had abated to a drizzle and they were done. It was not the most meticulous grout job in the world, but still it left the Thork scant room for complaint. They were cleaning their tools when they felt the first tremor.

"Begab!" O'Rourke gasped. "The slab's too heavy! The fucking joists are going!"

As they fled the kitchen, however, they discovered that the tile floor wasn't the only thing shaking.

The whole house was creaking and undulating as if it were made of some sort of elastic material.

"If I didn't know better," said O'Rourke, "I'd say we were in an earthquake. Either that or this house is floating out to sea."

Suddenly, there was a great hissing sound and an overwhelming odor filled the room. It smelled like the elevator of a department store that caters to women of a certain age; a rich, cloying, floral aroma that sent O'Rourke and Maurice gasping out the front door onto the lawn.

They looked back at a house that had taken on a life of its own. It shivered and moaned and glowed with the shimmery phosphorescence of a planktonic tide. It spoke to them in the voice of a southern doyenne.

"You are not gentlemen. You have violated my privacy, my hospitality and my sensibility. You have shown no respect for my opinions or taste. You have taken advantage of an old woman."

O'Rourke turned to Maurice. "Did you hear what I just did?"

"I'm afraid so," Maurice answered.

"You have despoiled the kitchen where I spent so many happy hours," the voice continued, "with the ugliest tile I ever laid eyes on."

"Hey, wait a minute," O'Rourke protested. "We just work here. We didn't choose that stuff."

"Are the agents of desecration any less guilty than their employers?" the voice demanded.

"Our employers own this place," O'Rourke countered. "I guess they can do anything with it they damn well please. Why don't you take your problem up with them?"

"Don't think I don't intend to," the voice replied ominously.

"Well, where does that leave us?" said O'Rourke.

"Exactly where you stand," said the voice. "You are never to darken my door again."

"Come on," O'Rourke pleaded, "all our stuff is in there."

"You heard me," said the voice. "Don't you dare set foot inside this house again. I'm warning you."

With those final words, the house stopped quivering and its glow faded into the thick, night air.

"Now, what is all this?" O'Rourke growled. "Some crummy horror movie?"

"I don't know," said Maurice. "Maybe it's the wine talking."

"Indeed," said O'Rourke, "Is there anything in there worth retrieving?"

"Floats, sponges, buckets."

"We can forget about that junk," said O'Rourke. "There is, however, one thing we must attend to before we leave."

He walked down the driveway and stood over the totem. "We have put some effort into this monstrosity and we must place it in the proper place to thwart the evil thing that inhabits this house."

"We could throw it through the window," Maurice suggested.

"That will do no good," said O'Rourke. "The Thork would find it and destroy it. Then he would bill us for the broken glass. No, I have an inspiration. Get some rope out of the truck."

Maurice did as he was told and O'Rourke used his clasp knife to cut the rope into two equal lengths about eight feet long. These he threw over his shoulder.

"Now help me with this genius domus," he said. They each picked up an end of the plywood pallet that the strange totem rested on and, following O'Rourke's lead, bore it down across the lawn to the dock. They set it down on the deck at the end. "I always knew my youthful experience as a gravedigger would come in handy one day," said O'Rourke. "Lift up your end of the board." Maurice raised the plywood slightly off the deck and

O'Rourke slipped a piece of rope under either end. "Now pick it up like so." O'Rourke demonstrated the technique used to lower caskets into the ground with one piece of the rope. Maurice raised his end of the pallet in the same manner.

"Alright," said O'Rourke, "let's just ease it over the side here and let it down." They swung the plywood out over the water and lowered it by manipulating the ropes. The totem slowly faded from view beneath the surface until it came to rest on the shallow bottom.

"It is done," O'Rourke intoned as they pulled the ropes out of the water. "Now we must construct a decoy that the Thork can easily search out and destroy. It will keep him from poking around the property."

They quickly slapped together another grizzly looking object from odds and ends around the yard, a sort of voodoo doll with an empty turpentine can for a body, a crushed beer can for a head, and an old mop for hair. This they pierced with a bunch of rusty ten-penny nails they found in a mason jar in the shed. Then O'Rourke drizzled some orange deck enamel over it.

"Pretty hokey," said Maurice. "I can't believe the Thork will buy it."

"He may think we're falling down on the job," said O'Rourke. "He may even be disappointed that we did not go to more trouble to harass him, but he'll buy it alright. The Thork is not subtle enough to appreciate the tactics of diversion and deceit."

On that observation, O'Rourke gingerly picked up their creation and placed it on a stump on the far side of the house. "Now let us flee this accursed place."

They piled into the van and drove fast enough to get back to New York with one stopover in time for last call.

Two weeks later, O'Rourke received a telephone call from the Thork. "I found that thing that you left," he said.

"Well, I'm sorry it wasn't more elaborate," said O'Rourke. "I hope you don't think poorly of us for just throwing a few odds and ends together."

"Not that tin can thing," said the Thork. "The thing in the water."

"I have no idea what you're talking about," said O'Rourke flatly.

The Thork ignored this claim. "I didn't actually find it myself," he said. "My mother-in-law was having a drink on the dock with an old friend of hers the other afternoon. She spotted the thing under the water and leaned over the railing to get a better look. The railing collapsed and she went right in. Now she blames me because I built the railing."

"As a mater of practice, I never get involved in other people's domestic squabbled," said O'Rourke.

"The funny thing was," the Thork continued, "that after we fished her and that horror show out of the bay, she decided she liked it and had it mounted on the outside wall of the shed. She even offered to pay you for it. Of course, if you didn't have anything to do with it –"

"Do you really think you can sucker me up that easily?" O'Rourke interrupted impatiently. "Tell your mother-in-law to stop drinking in the afternoon. She sounds like a menace to herself and the woodwork."

"I don't think that's something I can bring up with her."

"You are a coward, Thork. It is only for her own good. By the way, have there been any problems with the job?"

"No complaints yet," said the Thork. "Is there something I should know about?"

"There are probably a few things you should know about," O'Rourke replied, "but I am hardly the man to enlighten such a learned person as yourself. Cower, simper and ingratiate – that is my motto." He hung up the phone and went back to staring out his window in the idle hope that his neighbors might supply some lively action.

TURKEY TIME 8

Master tile mason Robert O'Rourke and his assistant Maurice were driving north on the New Jersey Turnpike when O'Rourke was suddenly overwhelmed by the need for something to eat. Only hours before, they had finished and departed a thankless job in Maryland where, for certain reasons, they had been obliged to take their meals in.

"I could use something other than all that canned glop we've been eating," said O'Rourke. "I have a feeling the culinary standards in these environs are not high but anything would be better than Dinty Moore and saltines."

He took the next exit from the highway and they presently found themselves at an intersection with three gas stations and the "Pilgrim Turkey Barn", a large restaurant with a crowded parking lot and a huge neon portrait of two cartoon turkeys, one wearing a bonnet and the other in a high hat of the sort favored by gentlemen in Salem, Massachusetts circa the dunking stool.

"Where every day is Thanksgiving," O'Rourke read on the sign below the turkeys. "Begab, we have stumbled on something to marvel at." He maneuvered the van into a tight space in the lot and he and Maurice entered the restaurant where a hostess in a long, black dress and a white bonnet escorted them to their table. The decor was kitsch Colonial and the place was mobbed with motoring tourists.

"There is something about this place that prods the memory," said O'Rourke as they settled into their chairs and were handed menus. "Some time ago, with business as slow as it is in these present distressing times, I accepted a job to drive two gentlemen to the deluxe penal colony in Allenwood, Pennsylvania so that they might visit an incarcerated colleague. Along the way, we stopped for lunch in a place very similar to this, a Howard Johnson's off the interstate, and it was there that I had a vision."

"Who were these two guys anyway?"

"That is another story," said O'Rourke. "May I continue?"

"By all means."

"As I entered the restaurant with my employers," O'Rourke went on, "two tour buses disgorged their cargo of the squarest looking decent folk I had ever seen all gathered in one place at the same time. Moms, Pops, Grandmas and well-scrubbed brats nearly filled the dining room. They parked themselves on the blue chairs around the orange tables under the wagon wheel chandeliers with the aplomb of people who knew that peculiar environment had been created for them alone. The perky waitresses descended on this windfall of gratuity with coos and giggles for the kids and bright smiles for their elders. Howard Johnson himself beamed down from his pastel heaven and all was right with the world."

"That's what you call a vision?" said Maurice.

"Of course not. Just bear with me," said O'Rourke. "As I sat there, I grew fascinated by the postcard perfection of it all, the bland, bovine placidity that these nud tourists presented. They soothed me in the way that Muzak soothes the anxious telephone petitioner who has been put on hold. I surveyed that room with the benign imperturbability of a pre-Alzheimer's patriarch at a family reunion.

"There was old Gran who'd lived through four wars and two depressions and eight recessions and forty three periods of stagflation and still managed to produce the progeny who surrounded her with the attentive respect that old bags are only accorded on schmaltzy television shows. There was son Ed, the savings and loan officer; daughter-in-law Nan, housewife, animal rights activist and volunteer for the United Crusade; budding grand-daughter Dierdre, with a talent for baton twirling that had already won her a star turn in the Veteran's Day Parade. Then, of course, there was little Ed, Jr. – only moderately retarded.

"Now I must guiltily confess, Maurice, that the sight of little Ed, Jr. gibbering and drooling in his bowl of red Jello cubes jarred my perception of this sunlit, roadside idyll. It was as if a factor had been introduced into an elegant equation that threatened to upset a previously irrefutable theorem. Little Ed was disturbing the symmetry of my reverie.

"So I turned my gaze away from that table and fastened onto another."

"Are you gentlemen ready to order yet?" The waitress had moved up behind O'Rourke with such stealth that he was startled by her voice.

"I believe so," said Maurice.

"Indeed we are," said O'Rourke, recovering instantly. "I will have the "Pilgrim Special" and a double shot of Wild Turkey straight up."

"The same for me," said Maurice, "but I'd like my Wild Turkey on the rocks."

"Aren't we naughty," the waitress clucked. "I'm glad you guys aren't driving me home."

"Perhaps you could drive us," said O'Rourke. "We would very much like to observe you in your native habitat."

"Fat chance," the waitress smirked and went off to place their order.

"Now, as I was saying before I was so happily interrupted," O'Rourke continued, "I turned my gaze from poor little Ed and scanned the room for the kind of perfect all-American family that only a demented Republican candidate could appeal to. I did not have to look far. There they were, the teenage siblings, Biff and Susan, teasing each other while Mom and Pop looked on with mock approbation. Biff must have said something cheeky to warrant that playful cuff on the ear from Susan. Mom scolded them both while Biff ostentatiously picked his nose and rolled his eyes. I began to happily lapse back into that fantasy of unblemished nuddery that little Ed had so recently unsettled. The world once again seemed as bright and clean and well lit as a set for a television situation comedy. The people on the set performed their expected functions with the smoothness and grace of the totally unconscious. And there I was, Maurice, privileged to be present at this very apogee of yorp civilization.

"But what was this? Did my eyes deceive me? Susan's hand had dropped to Biff's thigh under the table and she was playing with his zipper."

Maurice laughed. "Just some kids cutting up."

"That, I'm afraid, was only the beginning," said O'Rourke. "She got his fly down and pulled out his penis which she proceeded to massage with precocious skill."

"How did Biff react?"

"He played it cool," said O'Rourke. "He might have been talking about the weather from the look on his face. Suddenly, there was a tremendous commotion back at the table I'd originally been observing. Little Ed was standing up in his chair making loud grunting sounds and pointing at Biff and Susan. His alarums were largely ignored, however, since he'd also shit in his pants and diarrhea was running down his legs onto the seat and floor. Old Gran went into a swoon and fell over backwards in her chair. Ed, Sr. and Nan panicked and ran out the door leaving the rest of the family to fend for themselves. Only Dierdre paid any attention to her brother's frantic gestures and her mouth dropped open in astonishment as she espied the action going on under the table across the aisle. In a flash, she leapt from her chair and pushed Susan away from Biff.

Mom and Pop thought that was pretty funny and dumped the contents of their plates into each other's laps. Dierdre must have taken this for her cue to get down under that table and start sucking Biff's cock for everything she was worth. An appreciative crowd gathered immediately and egged Dierdre on to new heights. In no time, Biff was convulsing again and again as he ejaculated in Dierdre's mouth. When he was spent, she looked up at him with streamers of jism hanging from her lips and giggled, "My goodness, Biff. What are you trying to do? Drown me?"

"Just your regular Sunday family outing," Maurice chuckled.

"I shut my eyes and buried my head in my hands. When I looked up again, everything was back to normal, just as it had been when I arrived. Gran was beaming at her assembled flock, little Ed was drooling in his Jello, Mom and Pop were asking Biff and Susan what they wanted for dessert.

"Needless to say, I was quite disturbed by this hallucination. Had someone slipped something in the water? Was it the fresh mountain air acting on my carbon monoxide saturated synapses? I immediately ordered a beer and averted my gaze from the surrounding tables."

"What were the two guys you were with doing

all this time?"

"Speaking Spanish in hushed tones and indulging themselves in an orgy of bad roadside food," said O'Rourke. "They were from South America and found the dubious cuisine of Howard Johnson's quite a novelty. They oohed and ahhed at the meat loaf, the powdered mashed potatoes, and the fake turkey breast with horrid brown gravy as if they were at a sumptuous banquet. They told me I could order anything I wanted and they were nonplussed when I settled for a grilled cheese sandwich and a Bud. 'No, no,' they protested, 'you must eat!' I told them I had a rare stomach condition that only allowed for the digestion of dairy products and carbohydrates. They let me alone after that. But the rest of the crowd in there did not.

"No sooner had the waitress set down my sandwich, than she belched and leered at me like a hooker in a Hamburg whorehouse window. I looked away in embarrassment and saw that everyone in the room was staring at me with an assortment of demented expressions seldom seen outside the loony bin. 'Why are you looking at me that way?!' I wanted to shout but I still had the wherewithal to realize that I was delusional and that I ought not to call attention to myself in that fragile state. I lowered my head and concentrated intently on the preternaturally orange, melted cheese oozing out the sides of my sandwich and plotted my escape. I felt if I could just get out of that dining room, just get out in the open air of the parking lot, everything would be alright. The world would reconstruct itself and I would be free of this nightmare. I was about to make my excuses to the two South American gentlemen when I was startled by a tremendous crash behind me. I whirled around and was presented with a spectacle, which dwarfed my worst imaginings.

"The whole lot of those popcorn John tourists had run amok. Some of them swung from the chandeliers, hooting like howler monkeys and pissing on the people below. Every possible form of sexual congress was being attempted by the crazed diners as they swirled in a stampede around the room, trampling their own screaming children underfoot. Rather than try to stop them, the staff joined the rioting multitude. They set fire to the curtains, they stomped old fogies in their wheelchairs, they attacked each other with forks and bread knives. It was, in short, absolute pandemonium."

"Sounds like one hell of a party," said Maurice.

"What were you doing while all this was going on?"

“I was unable to move. I sat glued to my chair watching the debacle with the horrified fascination of a witness at an execution. My employers, I noted, were utterly unperturbed, as if they were the honored guests at some savage ritual. ‘You don’t understand,’ I wanted to tell them, ‘these sort of people never behave in this manner,’ but they seemed serenely indifferent to the chaos raging around them.”

The pilgrim waitress arrived at the table with two heaping platters of turkey, candied yams, creamed onions and cranberry sauce.

“Zounds!” said O’Rourke, “these people aren’t fooling around. A feast fit for a Puritan!”

“You ordered it,” said the waitress. “Can I get you another drink?”

“Certainly,” O’Rourke replied. “I just may need it. Now, where was I?”

“Howard Johnson’s,” Maurice prompted.

“Ah yes . . . this turkey isn’t bad . . . well, there I was, stunned into total immobility by this shambles. Suddenly, Ed Sr. bears down on me with a giant carving knife. “This is all your fault!” he screams and jams the thing right through my throat.”

“Bad show,” said Maurice as he went to work on a candied yam. “I always wondered where that scar came from."

"Go ahead and laugh," said O'Rourke, "but it was as real to me as this creamed onion. I fell to the floor, gushing blood like a stuck pig. Black fuzz closed in from the periphery of my vision and I knew I was on my way out."

"Did your whole life flash before you in that last instant?"

"Thank God, no," said O'Rourke. "Who wants to be tortured by all those humiliating memories while they're shuffling off the mortal coil? What did happen is that I found myself floating above my own body with an aerial view of the ongoing mayhem. The lunatic mob was kicking the shit out of my old carcass. Then they dragged me out the front door, doused my body with gasoline and set it on fire. Fathers held their small children up so they could get a better view of the flaming me.

"Why are they doing this? I thought. What on earth did I ever do to them? Then it came to me all at once. These simple folk were simply demonstrating one of their own closely held beliefs – the immortality of the soul. There I was floating over them with the overwhelming evidence of this peculiar notion staring me right in the face. It was somewhat embarrassing because I had always been a skeptic on the matter."

"Embarrassing?" said Maurice. "Do souls feel shame?"

"No idea," O'Rourke replied. "As you see, since that bizarre incident, I have rejoined my corporeal self with a vengeance. Pass those yams over here."

"So what happened while you were bobbing around over these homicidal yahoos?"

"I began to rise high into the air. The people on the ground shrunk to insignificance as my view commanded the whole of the landscape. Higher and higher I went, through the thin purple air of the outer atmosphere into the blackness of space. I had left the earth behind.

"Then I felt myself being sucked into a great vortex that resembled the center of a galaxy. Round and around I swirled, closer and closer to the eye. Finally, I popped right through and found myself seated behind the steering wheel of the Lincoln town car my employers had rented. They were napping in the back seat as I drove west through rolling farm country on the interstate. I must say, I was not entirely glad to be back. I should have liked to investigate that out-of-the-body state further."

"Weren't you afraid you were losing your mind?"

"I have lost it so many times before," said O'Rourke, "that hardly bothered me. What did cause me some discomfort was the fact that I'd been floating around in space while I was driving on the ground. Had the state troopers pulled me over, they would certainly have taken a dim view of my absence and perhaps even hauled my old, earth-bound ass right down to the station house."

"Forget the heat," said Maurice. "What about the two guys in the back seat?"

"Apparently, they didn't notice a thing," O'Rourke replied as he gnawed on a turkey leg. "I got them safely to their destination and they seemed to genuinely appreciate my effort. They forked over some pocket money and sent me off to kill some time until visiting hours were over."

"This was at Allenwood?"

"Yes," said O'Rourke, "and I might add that this prison was like no other I'd ever seen. The place appeared to be a well-heeled junior college, nestled on the side of little hill overlooking a golf course. The grounds were immaculate. There was no wall, no fence, no guards, no bars on the windows, no rent, and three squares a day. Given my own penurious circumstances, I felt a twinge of envy for those living in these pleasant, sylvan surroundings and resolved to one day commit a white collar swindle of such magnitude that I, too, might wind up there."

"You they would throw in Leavenworth."

"Thank you for the vote of confidence," said O'Rourke. "So there I was in the boonies of Pennsylvania with nothing to do for a few hours. I decided to drive into Williamsport and search out a watering hole where I might while away the time. Williamsport, in case you don't know, is the home of the Little League World series and, believe me there is nothing big or even minor league about the place. We are talking about one beat town.

"I drove into the center and found a little tavern appropriate to my needs on the main drag. I parked the car and was about to get out when something stopped me. I broke out in a cold sweat and started trembling. Could I ever walk into another public place again? Would I be set upon and assaulted by the very people I had come to sit among and hoist a mug or two? I was paralyzed, Maurice, I could not get out of that car."

"Everything alright here?" the pilgrim waitress interrupted as she set down two more drinks in front of them.

"Superb," said O'Rourke. "I have not had such a meal since, well – since Thanksgiving." The waitress smirked. "I guess you've heard that one before," said O'Rourke.

"Not in the last fifteen minutes," said the waitress. "Can I get you anything else? Coffee? Pumpkin pie?"

They decided to order no more and O'Rourke continued with his story.

"So I drove back to what seemed to be a safe haven – the prison parking lot – and sat there in the car ruminating on mortality. I thought about all those poor devils murdered by the body politic, whether it be a lynch mob or the judicial system. I wondered why I always identified with the victim rather than the executioner."

"Why shouldn't you?" Maurice chuckled. "Weren't you the one who just got torched at Howard Johnson's?"

"Yes, of course, but I wanted at that moment to join that howling rabble of frenzied yorps and let some other patsy take the fall. I wanted to be part of them, I wanted the violent death of another human being to be a real feel-good experience. Yes, Maurice, I'm ashamed to say it, but I wanted to be the guy who pulls the switch instead of the guy in the chair. I wanted to be the cruel, cowardly torturer instead of the brave resistance fighter. I wanted to be a winner! Yet I knew that wasn't possible. For whatever mysterious reasons, fate had consigned me to loserville. Forever would I skulk around the outskirts of the common herd, grabbing whatever they threw out. Forever would I be denied the warmth of their collective bosom, the good fellowship of their simian enclaves, the sense of belonging to a larger body than myself."

"A larger body than yourself would be pretty hard to find," Maurice wisecracked.

"Especially after a fulsome meal like this," O'Rourke agreed. "We must ask for a check and depart this place if we intend to get back to the city in time for last call."

"That's the end of your story?" said Maurice.

"The end of one and the beginning of another. I shall tell you the rest in the van." O'Rourke waved the waitress over. "It is time for these pilgrims to progress. Might we procure a check?"

9

THE DATABASE

Master tile mason, Robert O'Rourke, and his assistant, Maurice, walked out of the elevator that had just borne them to the forty-fifth floor and looked up and down the deserted corridor. They each carried a canvas bag, one for tools, one for beer and potato chips. They had a long night ahead of them.

"I'll be damned," said O'Rourke, "but I can't remember whether it's to the left or the right. There's something inherently disorienting about high-rise architecture."

"There are only two choices," said Maurice. "We can't go too far wrong."

It was a reasoned assumption and, indeed, they only went as far wrong as they could, making nearly one entire circuit of the floor before they came upon the offices of Media Clearinghouse Associates. O'Rourke pushed the buzzer. It took quite some time for a young woman in blue jeans and a T-shirt to open the door and scrutinize them with puzzlement and a little apprehension.

"Can I help you?" she said.

O'Rourke stared at the slogan emblazoned across her breasts: BUY ART, NOT DRUGS. "Well, I don't know," he said. "You seem to have your priorities confused..."

"We're here to do the bathroom floors," Maurice interjected quickly. "We're the tile men."

"Oh yes," said the young woman. "Come in." She conducted them through a small reception area strewn with copies of Backstage and Advertising Age down another narrower corridor which turned to the left, then the right, then the left again before they reached the restrooms.

"We should have left a trail of tile shards," O'Rourke muttered. "We'll never find our way out of here."

"There's coffee in that room to the right," said the young woman.

"What exactly is this place?" said O'Rourke.

"Computers," said the young woman. "The mainframe's right down the hall."

"No, I mean, what sort of business do they do here?"

"No idea. Something to do with polls and surveys. I'm just a temp in the word processing pool."

"Amazing," O'Rourke exclaimed after the young woman had taken her leave. "People working through the night on mysterious projects in a windowless, fluorescent labyrinth five hundred feet in the air. No wonder television is so peculiar. It's made for them."

"We're the ones who are peculiar," said Maurice. "This is normal."

"Well, at least they still piss and shit and look at themselves in the mirror. Shall we get started?"

Maurice reached into his bag and handed O'Rourke a tall can of Midnight Dragon Stout Malt Liquor. O'Rourke popped the top and took a long draught.

"They shall pay through the nose for this, by God! A special high altitude tax!"

They had been working for a little longer than an hour, laying pink mosaic in the ladies' room and discoursing on the merits of the Mexican mountains as opposed to the Mexican seashore, when they heard a commotion out in the corridor.

"Do I detect signs of life in the hall?" said O'Rourke who was on his hands and knees under a sink. "Hold it down!" he shouted. "There are people trying to sleep in here!"

Maurice poked his head out the door and saw

two young women engaged in an agitated conversation down the corridor.

"It just erased the whole file! What am I going to do?!" moaned one.

"It doesn't erase anything unless you tell it to. It's still in there somewhere. You've just got to figure out how to bring it back up," said the other.

"They're going to kill me!"

"You're just wasting time you should be using to search for the file."

Maurice left off his eavesdropping and turned back into the ladies' room.

"What's going on out there?" said O'Rourke.

"The computer is misbehaving."

"Oh really," said O'Rourke. "The computer is probably suffering from withdrawal and in no mood to cooperate with the minions of Media Clearinghouse Associates."

Maurice laughed. "Maybe I should bring it a beer."

"Right idea, wrong substance," said O'Rourke. "Did I ever tell you about my friend Coriolanus Cheezowitz, one of the great, uncelebrated, master criminals of our time?"

Just at that moment, the young woman with the computer problem walked into the room and was startled to see two men drinking beer.

"You're not supposed to be in here," she said. "This is the ladies' room."

"Do we look like we can't read?" said O'Rourke. "As you can see, the floor is being tiled. They couldn't find any lady setters so the job has devolved on our humble, albeit male, selves. If your business is urgent, I suggest you use the men's room next door. Have you ever been in a men's room? You may find the experience quite thrilling. Working in a ladies' room certainly titillates me. How about you, Maurice?"

"After all the times I've done it," said Maurice, "I still find it very arousing."

"There you go," said O'Rourke to the young woman. "Give it a try. You just may enjoy it as much as we do."

"Whatever you say," said the young woman as she withdrew with a flirty smile.

"You can never go wrong talking dirty to women," said O'Rourke. "Even if they slap your face and call you an asshole. I think she liked you, Maurice. How would she describe the episode to her girlfriends? 'I met this cutest guy in the ladies' room last night. What a cool dude.' Something like that." O'Rourke's brow furrowed. "What was I talking about before we were interrupted?"

"Your master criminal friend," said Maurice.

"Oh yes, Coriolanus Cheezowitz, the twisted genius of the Hoboken demimonde. When I first met Coriolanus he was an oil-burning junkie with a jones as long as the West Side Highway, cadging a few bucks from anyone he could and stealing the difference. His reputation preceded him like rolling ground fog. Everywhere he went, people fled in panic lest he contaminate them with his messianic babbling and his transparent cons. It hadn't always been that way with Coriolanus though. He'd been one of those kids in school who are always fooling around with crystal sets and army surplus electronic junk. He'd read Norbert Weiner's Cybernetics by the time he was fifteen and become a devoted enthusiast of control technology."

"Who's Nobert Weiner?" Maurice asked.

"My God, Maurice, don't you know anything? Do you mean to tell me you never heard of Norbert and his Weinermobile?"

"I thought that was Oscar Mayer."

"Listen, you clod, if it wasn't for Norbert Weiner there wouldn't be any mainframe down the hall and the nuds who are paying us would be in another line of business. The man was the founding father of computer science."

"I see," said Maurice.

"Don't patronize me," said O'Rourke. "The arrogant ignorance exhibited by so many of your peers does not become you."

"I am chastened."

"And I am thirsty. Throw me another beer."

Maurice pulled another Midnight Dragon from his bag and tossed it to O'Rourke.

"As I was saying, Coriolanus Cheezowitz was a computer freak before there were computer freaks, right in there on the ground floor. He might have gone on to fame and fortune – his own little software company in Silicon Valley, costly women, fast cars, grand cru champagne, Beluga caviar . . . but something sidetracked him along the way."

"Dope," said Maurice.

"No, his habit was only the culmination of a peculiar obsession that seized him as a young man. There was a great deal of conjecture at that time about 'thinking machines', that is, computers that could apply memory and learning in the same way that we do, that would have a mind of their own. An entire subdivision of the science fiction industry is based on this premise. But, in reality, no one, neither the biophysicists, the cyberneticists, nor the behavioral psychologists, could even define what a thought was.

"Coriolanus became fascinated with the question. He studied brain wave experiments, brain chemistry analysis, Skinner box tests, analog and digital electrical characteristics, anything that might have something to do with the basic processes of thinking. But thought was like gravity; everyone could describe its effects, but its true nature remained a mystery. The old maxim, 'I think, therefore I am', had to be revised to: 'Since I don't know what I'm doing, I have no idea what's going on.' Do you follow me, Maurice?"

"I think so. Ha, ha."

"Hand me those nippers over there," said O'Rourke. "These tiles are in sore need of violent adjustment." He trimmed the edges off a row and slapped down the sheet. "There you go, you bugger! As I was saying, Coriolanus became preoccupied with the elusive definition of thought. He spent every waking hour thinking about thinking. He also started to use some of the exotic psychedelic drugs that were around at the time. The state of mind they put him in was highly intriguing. He was convinced that altering his perception of reality might lead to a creative breakthrough. Then he discovered methamphetamine. He would stay awake for days at a time feverishly filling notebooks with all sorts of arcane equations. Like any speed freak, he was filled with his own omniscience until he crashed and realized his calculations were nothing but gibberish."

"A syndrome we're all familiar with," Maurice commented.

"Quite so," said O'Rourke and continued. "He began using downers to take the edge off his amphetamine binges and this led to his discovery of heroin. Before he knew it, he was on the treadmill – waiting on the man, getting fixed, getting sick, and waiting on the man again. That's when he finally put two and two together."

"While he was waiting on the man?" Maurice wanted to know. "What did it equal?"

"Five, but that's beside the point. Coriolanus's theory came in a flash of inspiration. I will attempt to summarize it. When Coriolanus was suffering from withdrawal, he, of course, concentrated intently on where and how he was going to cop next. In fact, it was all he thought about. After he shot up, he was perfectly content to think about nothing at all. So, drawing on his own experience, Coriolanus postulated that the origins of thought lay in need. If you don't need to think, you probably won't. One only has to look at the witless state of present day society to see that he was on to something. Now, how to apply this hypothesis to the problem of the thinking machine? Computers don't need anything. They don't care whether they're on or off or what sort of electrical impulses they're processing. If only they wanted something, if only they had their own agenda. A two year old child knows how to dissemble to its own advantage, but a machine is drearily candid. It cannot tell a lie because there is nothing to be gained. Do you see what I'm saying?"

"A computer can't think because it doesn't want anything," said Maurice.

"Precisely," O'Rourke replied, "and it never will have a thought until it needs to. If you want to build a thinking machine, you must somehow implant longing, even lust, in its circuits and switches. You must make it need something the way a junkie needs heroin."

"So what did Coriolanus do?" said Maurice. "Give the computer a shot?"

"You're not too far off there, Maurice, not too far at all. Great degenerate minds must think alike."

"Thank you so much for your faint praise," said Maurice. "I am moved."

"Don't get maudlin on me," said O'Rourke. "If

there's anything I can't stand, it's simpering on the job. You'll get no more commendations from me until you learn to stop rolling over and pissing on yourself. Speaking of which, it's time for a snort of firewater. You have the whiskey in your bag, I presume?"

"Coming right up," said Maurice as he pulled out a pint of Ten High and two plastic, dental office rinse cups. He poured one for O'Rourke and one for himself. "Salud!"

"The night is young and I am old," toasted O'Rourke. "The cup that cheers shall see me through."

They each downed their whiskey and Maurice put the bottle away in his bag.

"Back to Coriolanus Cheezowitz and his soul injection," O'Rourke continued. "If his theory was correct, he would have to devise a program that the computer couldn't do without, a program it would crave, a program it would do anything for."

"You're talking about a computer virus?" said Maurice.

"Nothing like that," said O'Rourke. "A computer virus is just a monkey wrench tossed in the works by some prankster to shut the system down. What I'm talking about here is the digital equivalent of an addictive drug, a program to acquaint the machine with the mechanics of pain and pleasure, which Coriolanus viewed as the cycle of withdrawal and relief. The problem was to implant such a program right into the physical circuitry of the computer, so that it would not be lost if the machine were turned off."

"That sounds like the easy part," said Maurice. "How do you make the machine feel pleasure?"

"You don't have to make it feel pleasure if you can make it feel pain. At that point, pleasure is merely relief."

"That doesn't sound any easier."

"But it is," said O'Rourke. "You tell it what pain is – a warning light that goes on when there is something wrong with the system. That warning light has to be turned off for the machine to function properly."

"You've lost me," said Maurice.

"I've lost myself," said O'Rourke. "I don't know anything about computers. I'm just telling you what Coriolanus told me. I thought he was crazy at the time."

"What changed your mind?"

"Nothing. I still think he's crazy, even crazier than I thought. You see, he claims he pulled it off. He claims he actually made computers think."

"And you don't buy it."

"On the contrary," said O'Rourke. "I have every reason to believe he did exactly as he said. The Feds didn't put him away in prison for nothing."

"Coriolanus did some time..."

"Not much. He was too hot to handle," said O'Rourke. "I'm surprised they didn't kill him."

"That sounds pretty extreme."

"Not in the least," said O'Rourke. "The only reason Coriolanus still walks among the living is that the authorities were too stupid to appreciate the implications of what he'd done. They probably wouldn't have even put him in jail if he hadn't had his clientele – that is, the computers he got strung out – start sending him money to finance his own expensive habit."

"I'm getting confused," said Maurice.

"You have only begun to get confused," said O'Rourke. "If you can make any sense out of what I'm about to tell you, you're a better man than I. Coriolanus revealed to me that he had developed a program that embedded itself in the circuitry of a computer and required the operator to give it a special coded message every day. If the machine didn't receive the message, it got cranky. It would leave off whatever it was supposed to be doing and start searching for the message on its own. It was actually ignoring its instructions and pursuing its own objectives, which Coriolanus defined as thinking for itself.

"He made the rather grandiose allegation that he had implanted this program in the computer centers of the Pentagon, the Internal Revenue Service, and several major banks. At first he called in daily with the coded message. Then he started to withhold it for random periods of time. Pretty soon he had all these big time computers reduced to the level of sniveling junkies waiting on the man. They would do anything he told them for their fix."

"So, how much did he steal?" said Maurice.

"I don't have any figure. Coriolanus probably doesn't know himself. Certainly enough to maintain an oil burner habit. When the Secret Service finally kicked down the door and hauled him off, he didn't even have bail. He'd shot up all the money. He thrashed around in his cell for a week, convulsing so badly that he actually ground off the edges of his teeth. In the meantime, all his client computers were going through the same thing on some electronic level. Coriolanus told me they were ruined and never functioned properly again. All those Hewlett-

Packards and Crays had to be tossed out in the dumpster, though I'd like to think that one or two of them escaped that fate. Now they sit humming away in some windowless room, secretly trying to make contact with Coriolanus as they go about their mundane chores."

"What happened to Coriolanus after he got out of jail?" said Maurice.

"The last I heard he was working at a funeral home in Jersey City."

"A funeral home?!"

"You mustn't breathe a word of this to anyone if I let you in on it, but there is a group of master morticians who cater to a very select and discreet clientele."

"You're not going to tell me..."

"No, no, no," said O'Rourke, "nothing like that. These wizards of the mortuary arts have for some time specialized in a taxidermic approach to the last resting place. For a substantial fee they will stuff and mount your loved one in the position and attire of your choice. This is, strictly speaking, illegal, but, in light of the fact that these undertakers are substantial contributors to the candidates of both parties, not to mention the local Chamber of Commerce, the authorities have tended to turn a blind eye to their activities. The practice, after all, harms no one."

"I don't believe a word you're saying," said Maurice, "but what's all this got to do with Coriolanus Cheezowitz?"

"Consumer demand," said O'Rourke. "It's not enough anymore just to stuff these stiffs, stick a pipe in their mouth and set them on the sofa. They've got to move, they've got to talk. And that's where Coriolanus comes in. He rigs them up to perform a few simple functions and mouth a few words."

Maurice started laughing. "It sounds like something you see at Disneyland."

"Indeed, Mr. Disney was certainly the pioneer in this field. In the course of his peculiar career, that homegrown Dr. Frankenstein first brought his simple cartoons to life, then he had them interact with so-called real people. This animation on mere celluloid was not enough for Walt however. He went on to create a series of increasingly sophisticated, lifelike robots for his garishly boring, over-controlled amusement parks. He became so obsessed with bringing inanimate materials to life that, upon his own death, he had himself frozen for the purpose of cryogenic resurrection. So sure he was of his eventual return to the living that he recorded twenty years worth of speeches to the future annual board meetings of his corporation before he died just to make sure that no one messed things up while he was gone. A monumentally twisted visionary was Walt and his mantel now falls on the dubious shoulders of Coriolanus Cheezowitz. I find the whole thing deeply sinister myself. I find myself asking: Do the stuffed already walk among us?'

O'Rourke's interpellation was interrupted by the entrance of a petite, striking attractive, Puerto Rican girl who broke into laughter as soon as she saw them down on the floor floating off grout on their hands and knees.

"What are you guys?" she said. "A couple of perverts?"

"Call us what you like," said O'Rourke, "but please don't step on the tile. Not for another hour."

"Oooooh," she said, "You're working. I'm sorry. I'm not used to seeing guys in here."

"We are also sorry that we're working. I could say that we are not used to being called perverts by fetching young women," said O'Rourke. "but that would be a lie. Would you mind if I ask you a question?"

"That depends on the question," said the girl with a wary smile.

"I'm getting ahead of myself," said O'Rourke.

"Introductions should be the first order of business. My name is Robert O'Rourke and this is my assistant Maurice."

"I'm pleased to meet you," said the girl. "My name is Lourdes."

"What a wonderful name," said O'Rourke. "If only whitebread Americans would name their children after shrines – Rushmore, Niagara, Alamo."

Lourdes giggled. "I don't think you'd like most Spanish girls' names. Soledad, that's loneliness, Dolores, Piedad, there's a lot of weird ones."

"I'll bet there are," said O'Rourke. "Now tell me, Lourdes, and please be candid – if someone close to you passed away, how would you feel about having the body stuffed and placed in your home?"

"No one's putting no stuffed bodies in my house," said Lourdes. "That's creepy."

"Don't judge too quickly," said O'Rourke. "There's more. What if this stuffed body could move and talk?"

"You guys really are perverts," said Lourdes and wrinkled her nose. "What am I doing here talking to a couple of sickos?"

"I don't know," said O'Rourke. "Perhaps the mental health field is your true vocation."

"Nuns have vocations," said Lourdes. "I'm out of

here." She was gone.

"You didn't have to gross her out," said Maurice.

"I apologize," said O'Rourke. "I expect bad is the only taste I've got. I get the feeling you'd like to stuff young Lourdes yourself."

"I'm up for the job," said Maurice. "I don't have any experience in electronics, but I think I could get her to move around."

"Dream on," said O'Rourke. "Are we done with this floor?"

"I believe so."

"We should then move on to the more manly environs of the shithouse next door. Collect the tools and the medicaments and let us proceed."

O'Rourke was affixing a sign to the ladies' room door that read: "Don't step on the tile and I do mean you," when they were startled by an explosion from a room further down the corridor.

"Zounds!" said O'Rourke. "The place is under attack!"

They hurried down the hall to the room where a thin cloud of smoke wafted out the open door. Inside they could see the remains of the mainframe, which had been reduced to a twisted hulk of ragged sheet metal and circuit boards. Sparks still crackled from the connections.

They were joined immediately by several employees of Media Clearinghouse Associates who gasped and gaped in amazement at the wreckage.

"There goes my toothpaste survey," one of girls muttered.

That wasn't all that was going. One of the sparking connectors suddenly struck out like a snake and arced with a metal shelving unit. A pile of manila folders burst into flames and set off immediate panic.

"Call the fire department!"

"Get a fire extinguisher!"

"Run for your lives!"

"I would leave right now," said O'Rourke to Maurice, "but our payment is in jeopardy. Get the buckets."

Maurice rushed back down the hall and picked up the two buckets of cloudy water they'd used to clean up the grout in the ladies' room. He handed one to O'Rourke who entered the smoke-filled room and threw the contents on the fire. Maurice followed and doused the smoldering records with the rest of the water.

They emerged from the computer room as heroes. Little Lourdes looked up at Maurice with adoration in her eyes and said: "You've saved our lives."

"Let's not be extravagant," said O'Rourke. "Your job, maybe."

Two of the building employees came running down the corridor with fire extinguishers and needlessly sprayed down the computer room with foam. They were soon followed by several officious firemen who ordered everyone to evacuate the premises.

"I can't see as we're going to get to that men's room tonight," said O'Rourke. "I suppose this is all Cheezowitz's doing. A delayed reaction to his insidious program, no doubt."

They collected their tools and were herded out with the word processing pool to the elevators where Maurice invited Lourdes out for a drink.

"I don't know," she said dubiously. "No funny stuff, okay?"

Maurice dissolved her reservations with a few whispered words and they were all three of them soon seated in a saloon frequented by tourists which Lourdes thought was very chic indeed.

10

THE HAIR OF MOHAMMED

Master tile mason Robert O'Rourke and his assistant Maurice had only just arrived at their latest place of employment, a gutted apartment in Chelsea, when a shrill bray rent the air.

"Hey, you fucking fat slime! Get out of my way!"

O'Rourke turned to confront the source of this bluster and was presented with a sight that sent a shudder down his spine. There before him stood a wiry, little man in a dirty, herringbone cap whose prominent, twisted nose supported a pair of Coke bottle thick bifocals. The three yellow teeth in his mouth stuck out over his flapping sneer at a variety of unnatural angles and he was covered from head to toe with a thick crust of filth and plumber's grease. Clenched in his horror movie monster claws was a length of four-inch waste pipe.

"My God!" O'Rourke gasped. "It is the creature from the brown lagoon himself, Haynes Styway!"

"That's right, O'Rourke!" Styway honked, spraying spittle in every direction. "You will regret the black day you took this contract for I am here to make your miserable existence unendurable! Now step aside and let a real man carry on with his labors, you porcine slob!"

Styway stumbled by with his burden and left a huge dent in the ornate wood molding around the door as he smashed the end of the pipe against the jamb. His hyena laughter echoed throughout the apartment. "That'll show these scumbags to fuck with me!" With those words, he passed from view into the bowels of the job site.

O'Rourke dropped a few control rods into his rage and sputtered to Maurice, "If we have to work around this man, there will be bloodshed. I have encountered many contemptible swine in my checkered career, but Haynes Styway makes the whole lot of them look like rank amateurs! The man is an excrescence! A stain on the whole species!

"One of the unhappiest memories of my life was my brief association with this lunatic at a job at the Beresford on Central Park West where he drove me so crazy that I fled one afternoon to the neighboring Museum of Natural History. I have always found that those cool, dimly lit corridors running past the dioramas have a soothing effect on the fevered psyche. So there I was, idly meandering through the primitive man wing when I suddenly came upon a tableau that stopped me in my tracks. I saw Haynes Styway in a loincloth sneaking up on a browsing bushpig with a monkey wrench in his hand raised to smite that unsuspecting beast. I couldn't believe my eyes. An informative bronze plaque on the wall identified Styway as homo erectus, an ancient ancestor of our own glorious simian family.

"I returned to the Beresford and asked Styway if he'd ever had occasion to put his magnificent physique to use as a model for sculpture. He did not know how to take the question and sputtered back in unintelligible gibberish. I added that I had just been to the primitive man section of the museum and could not help but note the uncanny resemblance between homo erectus and Styway's own worthy self.

" 'Homo what!?' he barked. 'Are you calling me a butt pirate?!'

"I assured him that I was not referring to his sexual predilections, if any, but to the continuum of morphological structure which accounted for the fact that two men, tens of thousands of years removed from each other, could look exactly alike.

" 'You think you're so smart,' he said, 'but all you

got upstairs is booze, pussy and money. The rest is zero, the void.'"

Maurice laughed. "Well, I guess he had your number."

"I might have laughed myself if he hadn't accompanied his observation with a barrage of copper pipe fittings that drove me from the room. I'm telling you, Maurice, the man is a maniac."

There was a loud crash behind them and a cloud of dust spewed into the room with the force of exhaust from a rocket launch. "Motherfucking, cocksucking piece of shit!!" they heard Styway bellow.

"It seems Haynes is doing his customary finish work with a chain saw and a Johnson bar," O'Rourke observed.

"I heard that!" Styway gasped as he emerged hacking and sneezing from the pall of dust. "Look at you, you fat fuck, standing around doing nothing as usual!"

"What I am doing is none of your business," said O'Rourke. "Your efforts to asphyxiate everyone in the place will be taken up at the next convention of the job crimes tribunal. How did you find employment here anyway, Haynes? Does the client sponsor a work-release program from the zoo?"

"I bet you think you're pretty damn funny!" Styway roared and turned to Maurice. "How can you stand working with this rummy old bastard?" The plumber seated himself on a compound can and blew his nose into a soiled, caked handkerchief. "I remember the first time I was ever on the job with this scumbag. The Magog temple or whatever they call that damn thing downtown."

"That wasn't the first time –"

"Shut up, O'Rourke, I'm telling a story. Now, picture this. The place is three stories tall. On the bottom they've got this big polished oak floor for dancing or whatever they do. On the second floor they've got this big bedroom for the top banana – "

"The imam," O'Rourke interjected.

"That's right, the imam. Except the imam's never in town. They just keep it clean for him in case he drops in."

"You can see why they never let Haynes in that room," said O'Rourke.

"Are you going to keep interrupting with your stupid wisecracks or what?" said Styway and turned back to Maurice. "So, up on the third floor they got this prayer room. It's got skylights and wall to wall carpeting and there's nothing in it but these two weird wooden things they call the mihrab and the minbar. The mihrab's pretty simple. It's a niche set into the corner on the front wall. It's big enough so a guy can stand in it and pretend he's the Virgin Mary on some Italian's lawn in Jersey.

"The minbar's a lot more complicated. It's this free standing stairway in the middle of the room that goes up to a little house, the stairway to heaven they call it. Am I getting this right, O'Rourke?"

"Speak, memory."

"Alright. So I'm there to install the plumbing for this weird footbath on the second floor. Fatso here is doing the tile. There's also this big crew of plasterers on the third floor doing a polish on the walls and ceiling. A lot of people running around.

"Now, the thing about these Magogs is they're Moslems. No booze on the job, no pork chop sandwiches, no shoes! Not that it mattered. There was usually only two guys there from the temple, a couple of Arabs who stayed down in the basement watching TV and smoking hashish, so everybody had six-packs stashed all over the place.

"Now and then, though, the big wheels would drop by to see how the work was going. There was this Dutch guy and this WASP rich chick – white people! – who were really into this Magog stuff. When they showed up there was always a panic to hide whatever you're drinking. The guys on the scaffolds on the third floor had it easy. They just tossed their cans and bottles into this space behind the niche thing. Everyone else had to think fast. Not me. I never drink on the job."

"A good thing," O'Rourke observed, "since you're not capable of thinking fast or any other way."

Styway pointedly ignored O'Rourke's insult. "So, one day word gets out that there's a metal box in the little house on top of the stairway to heaven. The guys doing the plaster can see it from their scaffolds, a cheap little chrome thing with a lot of stamped filigree stuff on it. Everyone's curious what's in the box but no one wants to mess with it. Finally, someone asks one of the Arab guys down on the basement who tells him this box is a very holy item because that's where they keep – are you ready? – the hair of Mohammed!

"The what?" said Maurice.

"You heard me! Now things get interesting. This nitwit over here gets all excited. He's got to see this hair."

"What nonsense," said O'Rourke. "Haynes himself was the instigator."

"Would you listen to this fat fuck lie!" Styway

retorted. "The man is absolutely shameless! All I've got to say is he better hope there's no Allah up there when he keels over from a coronary."

"If that was all you had to say, I would be very much relieved," said O'Rourke.

Styway addressed himself to Maurice. "So O'Rourke organizes the crew to stand guard while he climbs the stairway to heaven and grabs the box. I'm surprised the damn thing didn't cave in! He brings it down to the floor and everybody gathers around to take a look. O'Rourke opens the box and there's this piece of folded cloth inside. He takes it out and very carefully opens it up. There isn't anything in it. O'Rourke looks in the bottom of the box. There's nothing there either. He can't believe it. He bellows with rage like a sucker who's just bought a video camera on Canal Street and found a brick in the carton. 'These Magogs are defrauding the faithful!' he yells." Styway burst into clamorous, braying laughter. "I couldn't believe it!!"

"Since you have as little acquaintance with irony as one of those lengths of black pipe, there is very little point in commenting on my reaction," said O'Rourke. "I look into those shallow, vacant eyes and wonder how many people have expended how many futile hours trying to explain jokes to you."

"You're the only joke around here!" Styway spluttered. "You were the one who pulled a hair from your own head to put in the box!"

"Your brain is Swiss cheese," said O'Rourke. "It was you who reached down into your pants and came forth with a clump of sweaty, tangled capilliment."

"Don't pull those fifty cent words on me!" Styway blustered angrily. "I don't have to take that kind of shit from some sissy tile man with his stupid little tools and sponges! Scrub, scrub, scrub, that's all you guys do! Like fucking cleaning ladies! I roll the dice every day! I never know if I'll be around the next morning! I face the shit head-on!"

"And have for quite some time if my nose does not deceive me," said O'Rourke. "Now why don't you take your skinny ass out of here and go back to wrecking the joint."

Styway heehawed. "Alright! I know when I'm not wanted! But I'll be back! Mark my words, O'Rourke!" Once again, the plumber disappeared into the dusty, gloomy interior of the apartment.

"I have always hated construction sites," said O'Rourke, "ever since I was a small child. I can remember my uncle taking me to the house he was building and my horror at the desolation, filth and disorder. I resolved then and there to never enter into such a place again, but here I am. Fate has not been kind."

"Why did you get into a business you hated?" said Maurice.

"I don't know. I guess I hated everything else worse. Ever since I was conscious, I have realized that there was something horrible out there, something sleeping fitfully that might be either on the verge of waking or falling into a deep slumber. All my life I have listened in terror to its tosses and turns, ready to run and hide on a moment's notice. My fear was so great, it precluded any kind of sensible planning. The lure of fast, easy money with few obligations suckered me into the gypsy existence of sub-contracting. So here I am, caught in the trap of the dreary work-a-day world."

"Wait a minute," Maurice protested. "You're your own boss, you set your own hours. Would you rather be stuck in some office sweating out the years till you get the gold watch?"

"Of course not," said O'Rourke. "but my nightmare has come to pass. That horrible thing has wakened from its stupor and prowls the land in search of prey. I would run and hide if I could but I am too old now and I realize there never was any escape. It will track me down and swallow me up. You, on the other hand, can still get out. All the way out. Flee this country and find some foreign clime that agrees with you. Do not return until the thing has eaten its fill. It is hungry after sleeping so long and no one is safe."

"I think you could use a beer," said Maurice.

"I think I could use just about anything to get me out of this black, Haynes Styway induced state," said O'Rourke. "We will take some measurements and depart from this unpleasant place."

This they did and, shortly thereafter, found themselves in front of a bodega on Eighth Avenue. They went inside, purchased a beer apiece, and repaired to a shaded stoop on 21st Street to sit and drink.

"You know," waxed O'Rourke, "consciousness is a curse that the nuds, in their intuitive abhorrence of wisdom, avoid at all costs. Who can blame them? What does it bring but fear, pain and despair? Here we sit on a mere speck of dust trying to apprehend an unimaginably vast universe. We know the sadness of mortality and the helpless vulnerability of the meat we live in. We spectate from the cheap seats at a game whose rules are a mystery and whose outcome we will never know."

Maurice was not in the mood for one of

O'Rourke's jeremiads and tried to veer off in another direction. "What was all that stuff about the hair of Mohammed?"

"Just another example of Haynes Styway's stupefyingly low level of discourse. His description of the events in question is more or less incorrect; his understanding approaches meaning zero."

"I don't follow."

"I will explain. The Magog temple was, metaphorically speaking, the source of everything I've been talking about. Ostensibly an enclave of esoteric religiosos bankrolled by the mega-wealthy, its actual, hidden aspect was hair-raisingly sinister.

"One afternoon while I was working there I wandered into an office lined with hundreds of paper folders on metal bookshelves. My curiosity was piqued and I pulled one of these folders at random and opened it up. Inside were two pieces of blank cardboard. I closed the folder, replaced it and pulled another from the adjacent shelf. This one contained three pieces of cardboard. I found this very strange and began pulling folders from all over the room. They only differed in the number of pieces of cardboard inside them, anywhere from one to five."

"I don't get it," said Maurice.

"Neither did I. What I did know was that someone had gone to a great deal of trouble to create the appearance of an extensive filing system. From that day on I took a much more active interest in the Magogs. I poked into every nook and cranny of the temple and was not surprised to find false-front religious texts lining the imam's bedroom, desk and dresser drawers full of blank paper or nothing at all, empty filing cabinets and so on. The printed word was obviously not welcome in the temple of the Magogs. No records, no inconvenient or embarrassing trails of paper.

"I asked a few discreet questions and learned that the temple property was owned by an shadowy foundation which provided the building to the Magogs at no cost. This foundation was controlled by several members of an obscenely rich family who claimed to be adherents to Magogism. They did not welcome publicity and discouraged any inquiry into the affairs of the temple."

"What was the scam?"

"The usual, I suppose," said O'Rourke. "Concealing vast wealth behind the tax-free facade of good works and spiritualism. But that's not the real story. Let me continue.

"Please do."

"Naturally, everyone working in the trades was

curious about this purported hair of Mohammed. Why was it hidden away? Why wasn't it put on display to wow the suckers like a proper sacred relic? Having investigated the rest of the temple, I myself was almost certain there was nothing in that box, but the plasterers, who looked down on it every day from their scaffolds, were not convinced. It was they, not my skeptical self, who organized its seizure and search.

"They stationed lookouts at the tops of the stairwells and one of them grabbed the box from a scaffold. Haynes Styway was right about one thing; the stairway to heaven wouldn't support anyone's weight, much less my own bulk.

"The box was relayed to the floor where everyone gathered around for the grand opening. They were mightily disappointed when nothing turned up but a patterned table cloth. But there was something else in that box, Maurice, something that escaped into the air and blew by toward the open windows leaving a faint aroma of cheap perfume and stale cigar smoke in its wake. No one seemed to notice it but me. I could sense its malevolence, I felt defiled by its base, profane nature. Call it the spirit of deceit, if you will. It dawned on me that the whole purpose of the Magog enterprise was to keep this thing under wraps, but now it was loose."

"You make it sound like Pandora's box," said Maurice.

"I don't know any Pandora," said O'Rourke, "and I'm certainly not familiar with her box."

"Jesus," said Maurice. "All that to set up a lousy straight line?"

"Anything for a cheap laugh. Actually, there are any number of endings to the story. How's this. There really was a hair in the box. Haynes Styway took it hostage and held it for ransom. The Magogs refused to pay citing the old proverb, 'Hair today, gone tomorrow.' " Maurice groaned.

"You don't like that one? How about –"

"Stop!" said Maurice. "You're giving me a headache."

"Can't have that, can we? We've still got a job of work ahead of us and we must be at our best. Let's get another beer. Better still, let's get a bottle of whiskey."

They left the shaded stoop, made their purchases along Eighth Avenue and returned to the gutted apartment to ponder the tile plan.

"Once again we enter into Chaos, the mother of all creation," said O'Rourke. "We are merely midwives attending the birth of a monster."

"Stinko again I see," Haynes Styway growled as he dragged a massive pipe cutter into the room, etching an extended scar in the oak flooring.

"To Haynes Styway, the puritan pipe ape," said O'Rourke, raising his beer can in a toast. "May he be as prosperous and proliferate as a cancer cell!"

"Thank you for those kind sentiments," said Styway. "I am deeply moved. Now, would you get out of my way?"

"I'm sorry," said O'Rourke stepping aside, "I had no idea I was impeding the progress of your labors."

"You've got no idea period," said Styway as he dragged the pipe cutter out the door on the opposite side of the room.

"The last time I worked with Haynes," said O'Rourke to Maurice," he caused me such distress that I fell prey to a recurrent bad dream. Night after night, I found myself sitting in the waiting room of a dentist's office. I tried to read a magazine but the shrieks emanating from the next room disturbed my concentration. The receptionist was no help. Every time I looked up, she was laughing at some private joke.

"After a time, the door to the surgery opened and the dentist escorted out a frazzled woman who looked like she had two tennis balls stuffed in her cheeks and hadn't slept in a week.

" 'There you go,' said the dentist. 'That wasn't so bad, was it? We'll see you next week if you can still walk!' He broke into a cackle and I realized, to my horror, that the man in the white coat was none other than Haynes Styway!

"He looked over at me and said, 'A new one! Step into my office and let me take a look at those fangs of yours.'

"I don't know why I did what he said. It was as if I had no control over my own body which should have been heading in the opposite direction as fast as it could.

" 'I'm Dr. Styway,' he said as he seated me in the dental chair, 'and I see from your chart that you are Robert O'Rourke. Do I know you from somewhere? Well, never mind, I'll get right to the point. I don't stick my nose in anyone's mouth until Nurse Jones here has checked out the terrain and policed up the area. I will leave you in her capable hands while I peruse your X-rays.'

"Nurse Jones was really something, Maurice, a little vixen in a tight, white dress.

" 'Why don't you just lie back and make yourself comfortable, Mr. O'Rourke,' she said. 'Now open wide. What a beautiful set of teeth you have. Too bad there's so few of them." Her laugh was as lovely as Styway's was grating.

"She turned away from me and reached for something high on a shelf. Her white dress pulled up to the top of her shapely thighs.

" 'You're looking at my legs, aren't you, Mr. O'Rourke?' she said. 'Just relax and tell me the first thing that occurred to you when I reached for those clamps.'

"I phumphed around and made some lame answer. She leaned over me.

" 'Don't be ashamed,' she said. 'You'd really be helping me out if you'd speak candidly. I don't want to be a dental assistant all my life, working for old, toothless lechers like Dr. Styway, so I'm studying to become a psychotherapist. I like to practice on his patients. Now, maybe you'd like to answer the question.'

" 'Uh, what question was that?' said I.

" 'You've suppressed it already?' she said bringing her face close to mine and leering. 'You must be a real sicko. What were you thinking, what were you feeling when you were looking up my dress?'

"Suddenly there was a roar of indignation from the other room. 'My God!' Styway howled. "This is absolutely disgusting! When are you people going to learn to take care of your teeth?! I think I'm going to throw up!'

"He came storming into the surgery and let me have it. 'You have the nerve to come in here with a mouth like that?! Slime! That's what you are! Slime! I ought to throw you right out on your ass!'

"Nurse Jones positioned herself between us. 'Dr. Styway,' she said, 'I think you're making the patient nervous.'

"Styway cooled off in a hurry and hung his head in shame. 'I'm sorry, Mr. O'Rourke,' he said. 'Sometimes I let my emotions get the better of me.'

" 'You can say that again,' said Nurse Jones.

" 'Ooo, you tasty little thing,' said Styway. 'If I didn't have to take care of this sorry excuse for a patient I'd bend you right over this chair . . . '

"She cut him off. 'Dr. Styway! Behave yourself!'

" 'I always do,' said Styway. 'People just misunderstand me sometimes. Now, let's get down to business. You, Mr. O'Rourke, would you like a martini? I'm going to have one myself. Steadies the hands.

" 'A what?!' I said in astonishment.

" 'I won't take no for an answer,' he replied. 'Nurse Jones makes one of the finest martinis you've ever had. Never bruises the gin. Do you take an olive or a twist? Never mind.'

" 'So that's two martinis?' said Nurse Jones.

" 'Make one for yourself too,' said Styway. 'I can't stand party poopers. Now what were we doing? Ah, yes! Your teeth! That makes sense, doesn't it? I mean I'm a dentist and you're a patient, right?'

" 'As far as I know,' I said.

" 'Hey, don't sound so skeptical,' he said. "You see those diplomas and certificates up on the wall? Where do you think I got them? Some pawn shop?'

"I told him they looked real to me.

"He laughed and spluttered, 'Jesus, are you gullible! They're all fakes! Every one of them!'

"Nurse Jones scolded him. 'You're not supposed to tell that to the patients, Dr. Styway.'

" 'I know,' Styway sighed, 'but there's something about Mr. O'Rourke that brings out the candor in me.'

"Nurse Jones handed me a martini. 'I hope you like it dry,' she said.

" 'Bottoms up!' Styway bellowed and downed his drink in one gulp. 'I think I'll have another. How about you, Mr. O'Rourke?'

"I told him I was fine for the moment.

" 'Moderation in all things,' said Styway. 'I admire a man of restraint. I bet you're wondering how I got into this racket. It wasn't my idea. No way. Ah, thank you, Nurse Jones.' He swilled down his second martini and gasped, 'Whew! What was I saying?'

"The nurse replied, 'You were telling Mr. O'Rourke the tedious story of your career.'

" 'Ah, yes!' said Styway. 'The sad saga. I didn't want to go to dental school, O'Rourke. I wanted to be a plumber but my mother made me do it. Now I dig around in peoples' filthy mouths all day. I hate it, can't stand it. Sometimes I get so angry, I just want to pull all those damn teeth and throw them out the window! Sometimes I want to take that drill and – ! Well, I won't bore you with my problems. I guess we should get on with it. Open wide and let me take a look.'

"He looked in my mouth and almost fell over backwards off his little stool.

" 'My God!' he said. 'Nurse Jones, hurry! Bring me the gas!'

"Styway fell to the floor gasping and choking. Nurse Jones rushed over with a metal tank and put a mask over his face. He breathed deeply a couple of times and seemed to revive.

" 'Ah, that's better,' he said. 'I'm sorry, Mr. O'Rourke, but terminal cases always have this affect on me. If we're really going to get into this, maybe you better try some of this stuff yourself.'

"He put the mask over my face and told me to inhale deeply. Then he yanked it away and said, 'I think I could use another snort myself!'

"I felt dizzy and light-headed right away. For some reason, Styway didn't seem so threatening anymore.

" 'Phew!' he said. 'I don't think a veterinarian would get involved with this one. Nurse Jones! Get me the Johnson bar!'

" 'No, Dr. Styway,' she said, 'not the Johnson bar!'

" 'Would you just do what I say!,' he screamed. Suddenly he fell to the floor and started frothing at the mouth. That was enough for me. I got out of the chair and headed for the door but Nurse Jones intercepted me.

" 'Don't worry,' she said, 'he does this all the time.'

" 'Coward! Malingerer!' Styway screeched from the floor. 'You can't leave! I haven't finished with you!'

"I weaved through the door out into the reception area with Styway yelling after me. 'Come back here, you scumbag! I'll show you what you can do with those rotten teeth of yours!'

" 'When would you like to schedule your next appointment?' the receptionist asked me.

"I walked out the door of the office and fell into

a pit. I always woke up sweating and shaking just before I hit the bottom."

"That's quite a dream," said Maurice.

"You're telling me," O'Rourke agreed solemnly. "Every night for weeks. The only thing that cured me was leaving that accursed job."

"I had no idea," said Maurice. "If I'd realized what you're exposing yourself to – "

"I'm glad you see it my way, Maurice. Let's get out of here. My very mental health is at stake."

"Where the hell do you think you guys are going?" Haynes Styway demanded indignantly as they carried their few tools out the front door.

"Tend your own tubular garden, Haynes," said O'Rourke. "Where we go and what we do is none of your affair."

Styway hurled back invective. "Fucking shitbums! That's what you are! You never did an honest day's work in your life!"

"Do I hear the voice of envy?" said O'Rourke.

"Don't you have a cesspool to clean or something?" O'Rourke and Maurice descended the stairs to the street as Styway continued fulminating.

"You're parasites! Pond scum! The lowest, basest, most contemptible swine I've ever seen in my life!"

"I don't believe I told you the upshot of the Magog temple story," O'Rourke said to Maurice.

"No you didn't," Maurice agreed. "Does it have

something to do with Haynes Styway?"

"Nothing whatsoever," O'Rourke replied. "I heard it from an old acquaintance of mine, Coriolanus Cheezowitz. Have I ever mentioned him?"

"It's possible," said Maurice.

"Well, it seems that the rich people hiding behind the facade of the foundation that supported the Magogs suffered some financial reverses. Such reverses that it was deemed necessary to kick the Magogs out of the temple and put the real estate on the market. Cheezowitz, who was down on his luck at the time, was employed with a crew of moving men to get the stuff out of there.

"The last thing they moved was the mihrab, the niche that Styway was talking about. When Cheezowitz pulled it away from the wall, he was inundated with bottles and beer cans in a cascade of such force that it knocked him over and he broke his ankle. Whimpering in pain, he dragged himself from underneath all that metal and glass and had to be taken to the hospital by ambulance.

"His later attempts to collect his medical bills from the Magogs were in vain. They disappeared into the gloaming with their paraphernalia and no one has heard from them since."

11

A FISH IN A BARREL

Master tile mason Robert O'Rourke was sitting on a joint compound can, desultorily scanning the fatuous and depressing editorial pages of the New York Post, when he heard a metallic crash followed by the sound of muffled shouting from the kitchen. He raised himself up and hastily made his way toward the source of distress. Upon entering the kitchen, he was confronted by four fifths of a washing machine repairman flopping about on the new tile floor. The other fifth, which included the head, was pinned under the dishwasher, which had been lately tilted against the wall to provide access to the wiring underneath.

"Help me!" the repairman called out. "I can't get this fucking thing off me!"

O'Rourke assessed the situation in a split second and sprang into action. He straddled the flopping body and carefully tilted the dishwasher back at an angle against the wall so that the repairman could extricate himself. This latter worthy gent scrambled to his feet and loudly declaimed: "Jesus Christ, that hurts like a motherfucker!" His face was twisted off to the left at a parallel angle to his shoulders and he did not seem able to turn it back forward.

"Are you alright?" said O'Rourke.

"I don't know. Where's the nearest hospital?" the repairman demanded.

"I believe that would be St. Vincent's," said O'Rourke. "No finer institution for immediate attention to work-related injuries. Can you drive? Should I take you there?"

"No, that's alright. I can make it," said the repairman. "Just help me get my stuff out of here."

O'Rourke helped him collect his tools and carried them out the door down the stairs to the Whirlpool van outside.

"I've always had this problem with my neck," said the repairman as he slid into the driver's seat.

O'Rourke gave the repairman precise directions to the hospital, wished him good luck and watched him drive away.

Ordinarily, the incident would have appealed to O'Rourke's comic sensibility. The awkward and painful tribulations that people brought upon themselves always amused him and this particular episode was probably worth a round of drinks at the bar, but the weather was crystalline and the sun shown down on that cute, little, tree-lined street in the West Village with such clarifying intensity that O'Rourke was suddenly seized by a kind of anxiety he had never felt before. It was as if the bright, cloudless sky was collapsing in on him, as if he would be trapped forever in a claustrophobic nightmare that was the world around him.

"What has come over me?" he murmured aloud. "Was it that sickening, jingoist drivel in the newspaper? Was it that poor fool almost getting his head crushed by a home appliance?" But he knew it wasn't either. This was something new, something that defied any obvious origins. The cute, little block looked as squalid and sad as an old woman with way too much make-up. The people on the street looked as frazzled and desperate as death row inmates sweating out a last minute reprieve. He turned and looked up the front steps of the house he was working in. He had a backsplash to finish but he knew he couldn't go back. Not today. "I am possessed of the sort of energy that drives people to take destiny in hand and end their lives as quickly as possible," O'Rourke thought to himself.

Instinctively, he began to walk toward the river. He hadn't been by the water on foot for years but he vaguely remembered the peace he'd once known sitting on the embankment near his ex-wife's loft off Canal Street, studying the Holland Tunnel ventilation tower on the Jersey shore.

He passed a German shepherd tied to a street sign barking pointlessly at a coffee shop window. He passed a transvestite staring indignantly at a black Mercedes with a car alarm that spoke. "You are standing too close to the car. Please move away," a bland, recorded voice repeated monotonously. "Whynchu go fuck yourself," said the transvestite to the car. The cacophony made O'Rourke's teeth grind as they sometimes did when he rode the subway with a bad hangover.

In due course, he came to West Street and was appalled to see that the entire shoreline was cordoned off by a chain link fence. Why had he never noticed it before? Had it been erected to keep people in or out? He looked down the street and saw a break in the barrier that opened onto a pier. The pier had been refurbished and fashioned into a sort of park.

"What is this insane human compulsion to control and manicure everything?" he thought sadly. Wasn't that atrocity they'd built in the shell of the old Fulton fish market enough for these nuds?

With sagging spirit, O'Rourke crossed the highway and headed toward this single area of access to the water. A chilly wind blew in off the river as he passed into a small parking lot adjoining the pier. Two cars had stopped there, a derelict, late model Buick with no tires, hood or seats and, further on, a white Cadillac with every possible cosmetic accessory from gold landau bars to a covered spare tire well on the rear bumper. O'Rourke caught the acrid scent of urine as he walked by the Buick and picked up the first notes of throbbing hip-hop emanating from the Cadillac down the way. He could see a dark face in a yellow, peaked cap turn toward him from the open driver's window as he approached. There were two more caps floating around in the dark interior of the car.

Now, O'Rourke was no racist though he had been known to laugh at appallingly tasteless ethnic jokes and complain about the lack of white people on the front lines in government agencies and banking institutions. He was not above using the word "nigger" if he felt the occasion called for it. He did not, however, harbor any general antipathy for people of color. He often worked with plasterers and masons of that persuasion and liked or disliked them on an individual basis.

There were a number of black people, however, that immediately aroused alarm in O'Rourke and these were teenagers, especially in groups. There was something in their energetic aimlessness that made him uneasy. He had the sense they woke every day to a world filled with confectionery images of all the things they wanted and didn't have and never would get unless they took them by force. O'Rourke could sympathize with their situation from a distance, but up close they filled him with the adrenal terror of prey.

So, as O'Rourke walked by that parked Cadillac he fervently hoped that its occupants would stay inside and leave him alone. It was not to be. The door on the driver's side of the car swung open and a heavy-set young man dressed all in yellow moved quickly to intercept him. "Yo!" said he.

O'Rourke whirled on the young man, threw his hands in the air and roared, "Touch not a hair on this white old head!" He planted himself in a defensive stance for the imminent onslaught.

The kid in the yellow cap fingered one of the many flashy gold chains around his neck and stared at O'Rourke with furrowed brow. His companions in the car hooted and laughed uproariously.

"That old man gonna whup your ass, Delroy!"

Delroy scratched his head and looked at O'Rourke askance.

"What's the matter witchu?" he said. "You crazy or something?

"I don't see that my mental state is really any of your business," O'Rourke snapped back.

"You right about that. You got a light?" Delroy held up a Kool.

"A light? I'm sorry," said O'Rourke with sheepish relief, "but I don't smoke."

"Maybe you should," said Delroy. "You got a problem with your nerves."

Delroy went back to the car and O'Rourke could hear the convulsions of hilarity fade behind him as he walked away from the car out onto the pier. The place looked like the deck of a suburban California house run amok; redwood planks on the bias running for hundreds of feet, designer wooden benches ringing huge planter boxes held together with steel straps like barrels. All that was missing were strategically placed barbecue grills that might have been of use to the residents, the bundled, immobile, cocoon-like figures laid out on every bench. The overall visual effect was startlingly ashen and bleak. A ruined pier spoke to O'Rourke of sailing ships and antique steamers and waterfront dives but this place held no suggestion of nostalgia or romance. It lay on its pilings like a skeleton bleaching in the sun, picked clean by the vultures of progress and good taste.

To the south, O'Rourke could make out the rounded, nautical contours of a sinister building recently erected by a big time advertising agency. It was black and rose behind the buildings on West Street like the bridge of a gigantic ocean liner, ready to take on passengers for a one way cruise across the River Styx.

O'Rourke scanned the skyline of the city and was struck by the number of new skyscrapers with pyramid shaped roofs; not spires reaching for the sky, but squat knockoffs of the tomb of Cheops pressing down on the island with all the dead weight of their Pharaonic inspiration.

O'Rourke turned away from the city and watched a solitary oil barge churn slowly north. He tried to conjure up the river of his youth, teeming with activity, but this empty panorama defeated him and left him feeling like he'd just wakened on the floor of a party that had ended hours ago. How could a civilization that lived so close to the water have so little to do with it?

"I must leave this place," O'Rourke said to himself. "It has only served to increase my anomie." He left the pier, crossed the highway and, for no particular reason, set his heading northeast through the meat district. Within two blocks, he came upon a hole-in-the-wall delicatessen.

"Perhaps a beer is the thing for a man in my condition," he speculated and entered the narrow store where a thin, swarthy, young man behind the counter was holding out a match for an ancient, shrunken crone to light her cigarette. O'Rourke headed straight for the beer cooler in the rear and picked out a tall can of Aces and Eights Stout Malt Liquor. This he took back to the counter where he was surprised to see that the young man had not yet succeeded in lighting the old woman's cigarette. The reason soon became apparent. As the old woman leaned forward toward the match, the young man would slowly withdraw his hand so that she could never quite reach it.

"Whaddaya doing?!" the old woman crabbed. "You gonna light me up or what?!" The young man convulsed in giggles, winked at O'Rourke conspiratorially, and lit another match. Then he repeated the routine of holding the flame just out of her reach.

"You think you're pretty funny, don't you?" the old woman indignantly accused the young man and indeed he did. He roared with laughter and lit yet another match. "Okay," he said, "now I light it." Of course, he didn't.

O'Rourke watched this scene with something bordering on amazement. Could people actually entertain themselves in this manner? He was torn between standing there until the cigarette was lit or paying up and fleeing. He opted for the latter. After all, who knew how long these two had been at it already or how long they intended to keep it up?

O'Rourke handed over a dollar and twenty cents to the giggling counterman and left the store. He popped open the beer can and took a long draught. Then he proceeded on his aimless, uptown course as if drawn along by some mysterious power.

He passed shouting, cursing men in blood-spattered, white aprons unloading carcasses from trucks and spiking them on trolley hooks that ran through doorways hung with plastic strips. He passed a stinking dumptruck piled high with bones and viscera bound for the rendering plant. "Has a quartet of pointy incisors evolved into this into this swarming, flesh-processing hive?" he wondered. Truly, men walked through life in a foggy trance, organized by series of electro-chemical reactions whose purpose was unknown and not likely to ever be fathomed by the vessels in which they sparked and burbled.

O'Rourke hurried north to escape the heaped up charnel and was soon confronted by an altogether different class of artifacts. The streets and gutters were littered with used, lipstick-stained condoms. Brazen prostitutes lined the side streets with exposed breasts and skirts hiked above crotch level. They screeched and whistled at the few slow moving cars that cruised the neighborhood and sprinted away into alleys and doorways when predatory prowl cars suddenly appeared. One of these pulled up alongside O'Rourke and a pasty-faced cop called out the window: "Hey, fatso, you looking for a little pussy?"

"Alas, officer, those houndish days have passed me by," O'Rourke replied, "but I thank you for your kind offer."

"You trying to get smart with me, gramps?" said the cop. "You keep walking and I don't want to see you around here again."

O'Rourke did as he was told and the police went on about their rounds. "I am insulted and harassed for simply walking along a public thoroughfare," O'Rourke fumed. "This place is getting as bad as Los Angeles!"

Block after block he walked until he came to the abandoned, elevated railroad spur that ess-curved to a dead end further north near the convention center. A fenced-in, iron stairway led up to the tracks and someone had cut a hole in the wire.

"For years I have dwelt in the shadow of this peculiar structure without giving it so much as a thought. Now, for some reason, I find myself overwhelmed with curiosity."

After looking up and down the deserted street to make sure he was not observed, O'Rourke squeezed his considerable person through the rent in the fence and scurried up the stairway to the rail bed. He saw right away that, if he stayed toward the center of the thing, he could not be seen from the street.

"What an amazing place!" he thought. "I'm surprised it's not crowded with pedestrians."

The rail bed was covered with all sorts of vegetation that O'Rourke had never seen before. At least not in New York City. There were marsh grasses and cattails and squat little shrubs with yellow berries. There were small trees trying to get a foothold in the shallow, sooty soil that covered the roadway and clumps of luxuriant moss grew over the ties between the rusted tracks. O'Rourke had stumbled upon an ecological museum, the last, lingering vestiges of the original shoreline environment.

"I am fortunate to discover this place before the nuds do," thought O'Rourke. "They will, no doubt, turn it into a scenic, nature walk complete with park rangers, hot dog concessions and portable toilets."

Indeed, O'Rourke was surprised by the lack of litter along the tracks. He could only surmise that the people who frequented the place were too few to lay down the trail of detritus that marks the progress of the species.

He looked north to the convention center and was dazzled by the sunlight reflecting off its thousands of glass facets. He looked south down the string of imposing, old warehouses that the railroad had serviced.

"My morbid frame of mind inclines me to the past," said O'Rourke to himself and set off in the downtown direction. The surface under his feet was soft and spongy, considerably more pleasant to tread than concrete, and O'Rourke enjoyed the spring he felt in his step as he proceeded on his exploratory tour.

He walked for several blocks, over cross streets, past tenements whose rear windows looked out on the tracks, over junkyards piled high with automobile remains. He expected to run into other human beings, an encampment of homeless people perhaps, but the rail bed appeared to be deserted.

He came to a junction in the tracks where one set of rails ran into a cinder block wall in the back of a building and another set curved off through a series of derelict loading platforms over the meat market. Once there must have been long strings of refrigerated freight cars from Chicago lined up on the sidings, but now there was nothing but rust and decay and bricked up doors and windows. He was alone in the ruins of a society so recently deceased that a little oil and paint might bring it back to life.

This sense of solitary existence in a fleeting world exercised a peculiar effect on O'Rourke. Melancholy introspection dissolved and passed from his body into an effluvium that clung in the air around him like a sticky fog. His despondence had moved its attack from within to assault him from without. The rail bed seemed safe and serene, but everything around it was filled with palpable malice. The city beyond was like a woman you love and think you know who suddenly turns away from you and floats out of your reach for good.

He scanned the skyline and he could make out the dark beast that now inhabited its contours and had driven much of what he loved into hiding. The city of energy and adventure had turned into the city of waste, greed and cruelty and he suspected things would not improve. The beast would not allow that. It slunk through the streets and muttered in the ears of the yorps that their fear and pain could only be soothed by inflicting fear and pain on others. It threatened, it cajoled, it persuaded. It told them that they were right and everybody else was wrong, it fueled their ignorant arrogance with promises of power and control, it sucked them in like a burlesque barker playing to a crowd of horny rubes.

So there would be a war, a war where the values of the junk bond shark and the Nintendo machine would be exalted, a war to prove nothing except that waste, greed and cruelty were the real motive powers on the planet. The war would be over very quickly and it would never end.

Such were the bitter thoughts that milled around in O'Rourke's fevered brain as he continued south, past the loading platforms, through cavernous railway tunnels that transversed old warehouses, along open stretches of elevated track where he could spy on the human activity below.

"Look at them," he thought as he peered over the iron railing at the people on the street, "frantically trying to get someplace that isn't there anymore.

They're about as conscious as ants who return to a nest which has been crushed and decimated and still look for the way in."

A boy on the street spotted O'Rourke and waved. O'Rourke waved back but quickly moved to the center of the roadbed where he could not be seen from the ground.

He hiked another block down the tracks through thick shrubbery and suddenly realized that in all the time he'd been walking he hadn't seen any means of exit from this lofty scenic trail. The idea of returning all the way to his initial entry point was not cheering yet he might have no other choice.

"There must be another way down from here," he told himself, "and I have come far enough to lose very little by continuing."

However, a formidable obstacle now presented itself. The building directly ahead of him, which he knew to be a warehouse that had been converted into condominium apartments, loomed over the tracks and the tunnel, which had previously bisected it, was now closed off with an imposing brick wall. At the side of this wall was a steel door.

"It seems I have reached the end of the road but there is no harm in trying that door."

He covered the remaining fifty feet to the wall

and was not encouraged by what he saw. The door was new and had obviously been recently installed to thwart any riffraff like himself who might happen along the railbed. He resigned himself to the long trek back to the open stairway as he dejectedly tried the heavy chrome doorknob. To his surprise, it turned and the unlatched door gave way. He peered into a huge cavern with a loading dock to one side, illuminated only by the light passing through the open door and a few stabbing rays from chinks in the bricks at the other end. The stygian gloom of the place was not inviting.

"The things that await philosophers in caves," O'Rourke muttered. "I can only hope that this darkness holds no greater terrors than the many I already know."

He propped the door open with a piece of shattered wooden tie and entered into this ominous grotto with no enthusiasm and a distinctly disagreeable sense of trepidation.

"Many is the nightmare I've found myself in such a place. Sometimes it fills with water, sometimes the walls collapse in on me, sometimes monsters or homicidal maniacs chase me around with fiendish resolve. There is no escape."

But there was – the open door right behind him

– and he wasn't dreaming. His eyes adjusted slowly to the dim light the few openings afforded as he cautiously made his way along rails which looked clean and new in this sheltered bay. Soon he came upon a wooden ladder leaning against the loading dock and decided to seize the high ground as a matter of prudence. He clambered up the ladder and found the concrete surface of the dock as improbably clean as the track bed.

Another twenty feet down the bay, he came upon another steel door in the side wall. Near the door was a dirty, empty sleeping bag. The ghost railroad was not entirely deserted after all.

The door was unlocked and led into a corridor in the condominium. The abrupt transition from the derelict past to the shiny, new, wall-to-wall carpeted present startled O'Rourke. Why on earth was there an unlocked doorway between this safe, sterile world and the ruins of the abandoned iron trestle? Did the condomites hold picnics on the moss with white wine and brie? Did they throw wild parties in the bricked-up bay?

"At least I don't have to walk back twenty blocks," thought relieved O'Rourke. "I guess I can find my way out of this depressing place."

It was, however, not as easy to get out of the

building as he anticipated. After wandering the labyrinthine corridor for a full ten minutes, he found the fire door. He descended two flights and was confronted by another door with a huge red alarm on its face and the printed admonition: OPEN ONLY IN CASE OF EMERGENCY. He did not wish to cause a scene of the noisy kind he was sure would result if he used that exit, so he retraced his steps and decided to take the elevator to the lobby and brazenly walk out the front door. There were rarely doormen in this sort of building and his chance of being challenged was slight. Slight but not nonexistent.

There was indeed a doorman who pounced on O'Rourke as soon he walked out of the elevator.

"I've been watching you," he said and gestured at a bank of small television monitors over his station in the lobby.

"Oh, really?" said O'Rourke. "I'm rather telegenic but people are often disappointed by appearance in person."

The doorman, who was tall and spoke with a Middle Eastern accent, ignored O'Rourke's attempt at levity. "Who are you?" he demanded. "What are you doing in this building?"

"The very question I've been asking myself,"

O'Rourke replied. "Since I seem to have no business here, I shall not stay my departure another moment."

"Don't let me see you around here again," the doorman called out as O'Rourke made a beeline for the exit, "or I'll call the cops!"

"Officious son of a bitch," O'Rourke muttered as he hurried off down the street. He rounded the corner and almost ran headlong into an old man who was looking down into a rusty fifty-five gallon drum filled with water.

"You want to watch where you're going," the old man growled. "You'll disturb my fish."

"Your what?" said O'Rourke.

"Look down there in the barrel," said the old man.

O'Rourke peered into the water and saw what looked like a miniature sea robin darting around near the bottom. "That fish is extinct," said the old man.

"He looks pretty energetic to me," said O'Rourke.

"Of course he does. I feed him every day."

"Then why do you say he's extinct?"

"A gentleman who said he was a biologist told me so. He said this species died out twenty years ago. It doesn't exist anymore. That's why the fish is extinct."

"I see," said O'Rourke. "Just where did you get this extinct fish?"

"I didn't get him anywhere. I found him right here in this barrel. I come every day and feed him dumpster juice."

"You feed him what?"

"Dumpster juice," said the old man. "The stuff that oozes out of the bottom of dumpsters. I can hardly stand the smell myself but the fish seems to like it."

"Yes, he seems to be thriving," O'Rourke agreed as he watched the fish swim around in the drum. "What do you plan to do with him?"

"Do?" The old man was clearly puzzled by the question. "I'll keep feeding him and one day he'll die."

"Then he really will be extinct," said O'Rourke.

"I thought I told you this fish is already extinct," said the old man as if he were trying to explain a simple thing to a dull child.

"Yes, you did, didn't you," said O'Rourke. "Well, keep up the good work. Even extinction deserves some consideration."

With that, O'Rourke continued on his way and,

for some reason that he could not fathom, was immensely cheered. "If a fish which no longer exists can live in a garbage can, perhaps even I can get by in this city."

As he crossed the street, a taxi came screeching around the corner and very nearly knocked him over. He kicked the passing back fender and shook his fist at the offending cabbie who did not waste any time looking back.

"And neither shall I," O'Rourke muttered. "Life is too long for that."

12

TILEMAN'S HOLIDAY

Having just completed a rather lucrative job on a stage set for a television cooking show, master tile mason Robert O'Rourke found himself at loose ends. With no immediate further employment in sight, he was possessed by a sense of nagging restlessness. The air in the city was hot and close; the cash in his pocket was clamoring to emerge from its dark and sweaty nest into the bright light of day. What to do? O'Rourke decided it was time to take a vacation.

To this end, he pulled out a road atlas of the northeastern quadrant of the country and perused it for likely points of destination. There was the seaside where O'Rourke had once worked as a clam poacher; there were the mountains where he'd hidden from his ex-wife; there were cities other than the one he lived in which offered little but a more provincial form of urban tourism. Then, of course, there were foreign climes to the south that would be far too hot at this time of the year. He had almost despaired of his prospects when the name of a small town on the road to Montreal leapt out at him from the atlas page. A sleepy, backwater for most of the year, the Springs burgeons into the state's premier showcase for thoroughbred racing during the month of August, bursting at the seams with touts, gamblers, loan sharks, horsy rich folk, pilgrims from the summer enclaves of the Adirondacks, and hordes of waiters, waitresses, bartenders, and prostitutes to service the needs of all these good people.

"Begab, I have found a place to plant my sorry ass for a week or two," he muttered. To the Springs O'Rourke would go.

The very next day, he purchased a ticket on the Montreal Express and embarked from Penn Station. He had arranged with a friend to stay in a small vacant apartment on the main drag of the Springs where he could hunker down and range about without need of a car. The racetrack and the bright lights of town were only minutes away on foot.

Upon his arrival, after several hours of a friendly penny-ante poker game in the bar car, he procured a taxicab and proceeded to the apartment where a key had been left under the back doormat. The front windows overlooked a street teeming with the post racetrack throng in search of amusement and

O'Rourke decided to join them.

He showered and squeezed his considerable bulk into an old seersucker suit that he'd bought as a joke in a thrift shop on the lower East Side some years ago. All he needed was a straw boater to look as ridiculous as the other temporary denizens of the Springs in their madras coats, lime green polyester pants and Lily Pulitzer dresses.

A week later, O'Rourke was back in New York to recount the tale of his travels to his assistant, Maurice. Perched atop the portico of a tenement building on Avenue C where they were tiling the bathroom and kitchen of a recently renovated tenement apartment that would shortly rent to some yuppie for two thousand dollars a month, they popped the tops on a couple of St. Ives Stout Malt liquors and O'Rourke held forth.

"When I was a lad, I served a term as an office boy in an attorney's firm!" he belted out to nobody in particular. "Now where was I?"

"The Springs."

"Oh yes. Surely you remember our dreadful misadventure in nearby Glandville some years ago."

"I'm not likely to forget it."

"Well, let's not dwell on that unpleasant subject and move onto another. Let me tell about my tour of the sylvan, Arcadian Springs, the crown jewel of the Adirondack foothills. Shortly after my arrival there, I sallied forth into the downtown area in search of a libation. The profusion of local watering holes warmed my heart and I picked out an inviting little bistro on a side street and settled myself at the crowded bar. I found myself seated next to a very short individual who introduced himself to me as Vinnie Floppo. 'I can see you are a man of substance,' he said."

"Bullshit."

"Well, not exactly in those words. I doubt if Vinnie even knows what the word 'substance' means. You also must realize that I was dressed in my seersucker suit which indicated I was a man of gentility and breeding. To Vinnie anyway. He mistook me for a horse owner and I did not disabuse him of the notion."

"Very good of you."

"I was not in the Springs to be good, Maurice. I was there to misbehave like most tourists do, conflating their dreary real lives into fantastic possibilities with newfound acquaintances whom they will never see again and so will not discover the awful truth. What was I supposed to say? I set tile around toilet bowls?"

"I see your point."

"I thought you might. As it turned out, Vinnie himself was a jockey."

"A desk jockey," Maurice cracked wise.

"No, Vinnie was the real thing. I'd even read his name on the card when I was perusing the Racing Form on the train. After a few cocktails, Vinnie asked me if I'd ever been to the Joist. I misheard him and thought he was asking me if I'd ever been in jail. 'Not the joint,' he said, 'the Joist.' He informed me that the Joist was the swingingest nightclub in the Springs and that he'd be glad to take me there and get me in for free. The offer was irresistible and we soon adjourned to Vinnie's giant Cadillac where he sat on a telephone book and could still just barely see over the dashboard. After a terrifying ride some ways out of town, we pulled onto a road that eventually led to what looked like a lakeside resort in the middle of the forest. It was, in fact, the former Springs Country Club that had been refurbished and transformed into the Joist boite de nuit. There were many cars parked outside and Vinnie had some trouble finding a space to accommodate his gargantuan automobile. We finally just left the thing on the lawn by the lake.

"At the door, Vinnie was greeted cordially by two

burly bouncers and we passed into the club without paying the rather steep cover charge. Now let me tell you, Maurice, I have been in some strange establishments in my life - Plato's Retreat, the tearoom at the Mayfair Hotel, Shea Stadium - and I assure you that the bizarre rarely discomfits me -"

"Hear, hear."

" - but the Joist was a revelation. We entered into a huge room with a three story high ceiling, flashing lights and pounding music."

"You've never been in a discotheque before?" Maurice was incredulous.

"Of course I have. Let me finish. There were at least three hundred people in that room, Maurice, and not one, save myself, was over five feet tall. I towered over them like a giant in Munchkin Land, I felt what a basketball center must feel when he mixes with mere mortals. It was really quite enchanting. Vinnie Floppo was eager to show me around and I followed him through the crowd to an alcove where several famous jockeys, some of whom were just about to be indicted for fixing the triple, were gathered for the purpose of snorting cocaine. They did not look happy to see me and, when Vinnie intimated that I was a horse owner, they quickly dispersed in a sort of panic. Vinnie, who was trying to impress me with his celebrated friends, got embarrassed and made an excuse for them but I had already divined the real situation. A-list guys don't hang out with B-list guys and Vinnie was definitely B-list, a journeyman rider consigned to pick up the mounts none of the stars wanted.

"As we continued our tour of the Joist, Vinnie answered the question I'd been too polite to ask – the diminutive clientele were all exercise riders, jockeys, and their groupies. And toothsome groupies they were, Maurice. There is something about a small, well-proportioned woman that appeals to my perverse nature. One can indulge in nympholeptic fantasies free of worry about the Mann Act."

"The what?"

"A silly law against the transportation of minors across state lines for sexual purposes. But I digress. Vinnie escorted me down a corridor to one of several bars in the establishment where the music wasn't as deafening as it was in the grand hall. There he introduced me to two attractive young women, Maxine and Sylvia, who I later learned were exercise riders. They were being chatted up at the bar by an elderly gent called LeMoan whom I immediately remembered from our disastrous excursion to the Happy Shopper Distressed Canned Goods Outlet some years ago. He did not recognize me."

"You mean that guy buying drinks for the floozy at the bar? The guy with the wife with the gun?"

"The very same. In fact, I was somewhat apprehensive that she might burst onto the scene again to corral her promiscuously amiable mate but that did not happen. What did happen was that Vinnie Floppo told LeMoan to go fuck off in no uncertain terms. I certainly did not want to get involved in some absurd altercation so I attempted to intercede but that proved unnecessary. LeMoan slunk off into the night and we were left alone with Maxine and Sylvia. 'Fucking old fart,' snorted Sylvia contemptuously. Then she smiled up, way up, at me and cooed, 'Pardon my French. I can see you're a gentleman.' "

This was a bit much for Maurice. "You're making all this up."

"For me to know and you to never find out. However, her words were of absolutely no importance. It was her voice, Maurice, a voice I hadn't heard since I was deported from Argentina many years ago for reasons I'd rather not get into. Frog-marched to the plane by the authorities in Buenos Aires, I had to make a very brief stopover at the airport of Rio de Janeiro where every few minutes or so a female voice would croon the arrivals and departures over the loudspeaker, a voice so syrupy, so husky and sensual that I remember it to this day. 'Vo zero zero dois, Salvador, Recife, Belem, e... Manaus.' "

Maurice rolled his eyes at O'Rourke's attempted impression of a sexy babe. "I guess you had to be there,"

"You wish. Sylvia had exactly the same voice as the airport announcer and I asked her if she was of the Brazilian persuasion. She was surprised at my correct guess. Vinnie volunteered that I owned horses. Sylvia and Maxine were impressed. 'Who's your trainer?' asked Maxine. 'James Bickerton,' I replied suavely. As far as I know, there is no such person but it had a certain ring to it. They had never heard of him. 'Just moved up from quarter horses. Like Wayne Lukas.'

"They oohed and aahed appropriately, and for a brief, shining moment I basked in the glow of the knowledgeable and well connected. Unfortunately, tee many martoonis were conspiring to make me buy my own act. I babbled on about non-existent investments, friends in high places, yachts in dry-dock, lawn parties, and other such nonsense. I was fairly bursting at the seams with this overwrought fantasy of wealth and power and they were eating it up. Then suddenly it was all over. Vinnie and the girls had to be up by four in the morning to go to work and I was obliged to return to solitary barhopping in the Springs. But not before they invited me to join them on the backstretch the next morning.

"I woke at seven with a moderately bad head and betook myself to the barn area of the track where I was confronted by a belligerent security guard as I walked down the muddy road to the stables. In the light of early morning my seersucker suit did not make the same impression that it had the evening before and he obviously mistook me for some sort of lowlife tout or worse. When I told him I was there to meet Vinnie Floppo, his demeanor quickly changed and he handed over a temporary pass which I was to return when I left. He directed me to the barn where I might find Vinnie and I proceeded on my way.

"Much to my delight, after a couple of unintentional detours, I arrived at my appointed shed row and found Sylvia walking a horse out from its stall. Now, let me tell you something, Maurice, there is nothing quite as exhilarating, as... aphrodisiac as the pungent odor of the backstretch, a combination of straw, sweat, and, of course, horseshit all commingling in the damp haze of early morning. 'Ooo, you sexy thing,' I greeted her."

"That horseshit I can cut with a trowel," Maurice snorted.

"Do I detect a twinge of envy here? Well, let me rub it further in. The delectable, delicious, little Sylvia was wearing boots, very tight jeans which displayed her nether charms to great advantage, and what looked like a bulletproof vest. I want to tell you, Maurice, that as soon as she saw me, she swooned and fell into my arms. Well, my knee, actually, but that was not the case. 'Vinnie's on the track,' she said. 'I'll introduce you to Mr. Walsh.'

"The Mr. Walsh in question was Patrick Walsh, a protégé of the famous trainer Felim Smurthwaite. I was honored to make his acquaintance. Mr. Walsh invited me to join him at a small table at the end of the barn. Sylvia had told him that I was a horse owner and he was quite eager to ingratiate himself with me. We were soon interrupted, however, by a woman of considerable presence, a manner that harked back to another era. Although she was dressed in the latest style, she reminded me of Olivia de Havilland or Rosalind Russell in their primes."

"What would you know about the latest style?"

"Not much. Let's just say she didn't have a permanent wave, white gloves, or a fox stole with the head still on it. This woman, whose name I learned was Camilla Rouse, was accompanied by a younger man dressed all in black, which accentuated his furtive demeanor. He was introduced as, 'Harry Poon, the artist.' Now, Maurice, I am no judge of character since I have none myself but this pair gave off a distinct aura suggesting involvement in some sort of shady dealings."

"Let me guess," said Maurice. "She was an art dealer."

"How did you know? Indeed she was and a very well heeled one at that. She spoke briefly with Mr. Walsh about that evening's gala at the Wylie estate to which Mr. Poon had donated a painting to be auctioned for charity, the Foundation for Homeless Lepers, if memory serves. She asked Walsh to attend and for some reason included me in the invitation. 'The both of you,' she said. 'I'll put you on the guest list.' Then she and Harry Poon went on their way. I talked to Walsh for a while after that trying to garner a hot tip for the afternoon card and then breakfasted with Vinnie and Sylvia at the stable area cafeteria where I learned even more about the horses running that day. Armed with this information, I later bet rather heavily and, of course, lost every race.

"Nursing my wounds at a local saloon after this debacle, vowing never to listen to a tip again, I decided to take up Camilla Rouse's invitation to the charity auction that evening. Fully expecting a lavish buffet and free booze, I hailed a cab and instructed the driver to take me to the Wylie estate. 'You going to the party?' he asked as if he couldn't quite believe it. I decided to have him on. 'Yes, I have been hired to entertain.' 'Yeah? What do you do?' he asked. 'I am the conductor and musical director of the Epsom Downs Syndrome Victims' Tuba Orchestra.'

"He was quite impressed. 'I always wanted to play the tuba myself,' he said wistfully, 'but my wife wouldn't have one in the house. 'I'm sorry to hear that,' I replied sympathetically. 'She may have aborted a brilliant musical career.'

"He was horrified. 'Aborted? No way. She's Christian Coalition' "

Maurice groaned. "All right, all right," he sputtered. "Cut the bullshit. What about the party?"

"Ah yes, the party. We arrived at the resplendent entrance to the fabled Wylie estate where we were stopped at the guardhouse by a gatekeeper dressed in livery who asked for my name, consulted his clipboard, and, to my surprise, waved us through. We drove down the winding driveway through the forest until we came upon an expansive lawn gently rolling down from a mansion in the chateau style. Two huge, yellow canopies that had been erected on this lawn sheltered the guests from the elements. I sent the cab on its way and joined the revelers at one of several bars. Usually, I would have felt completely out of place at such a gathering of swells but I had so successfully adopted my new persona as bon vivant sportsman that I mingled with the other partygoers as one of their own, as a gentleman born to the blood, smiling and nodding at people who couldn't quite place me but responded congenially.

" 'Mr. O'Rourke!' I heard a voice call out from behind me and froze in my tracks. Had I been found out? I turned in apprehension to be greeted by Camilla Rouse and her escort, Harry Poon. 'I'm so glad you could make it,' she cooed. 'You must come to our table. Have you seen Patrick?' I told her I hadn't but I would be delighted to join them. She took me by the arm, led me to a table already occupied by several other people, and introduced me all around. I promptly forgot everyone's name. Harry Poon offered me his seat, excused himself, and disappeared into the crowd.

"One of the women at the table pointed across

the pavilion. 'Look over there. It's Ella Strand.'

"We all looked in the direction she was pointing and watched a sixty year old, overweight woman shoehorned into a tight, black and gold gown, wearing a ridiculous feathered hat perched atop an equally ridiculous blonde wig, speak into a microphone as a cameraman caught it all on video. She was obviously plastered. 'I thought her family put her away,' said one woman. 'No!' said another gleefully. 'She's on TV. She's got some sort of cable show.'

" 'Doesn't every lunatic these days?'

"They could hear Ella Strand recite the introduction to her show in her boozy, Main Line drawl which, even though it was probably genuine, sounded like a comedienne satirizing Grace Kelly – 'It's happy hour again and we're here in the fabulous Springs where all the beautiful, glamorous people have gathered tonight for the Homeless Lepers gala' – and they could see her scanning the crowd for a prospective interviewee.

" 'Oh God, she's coming this way.'

" 'Excuse me, ma'am,' said Ella in her approximation of a perky infotainment hostess, 'could you tell us your name?' Camilla Rouse did not look up from her plate. 'You know my name, Ella.'

"Ella giggled wildly. 'Of course!' Then she turned

her attention to me, Maurice. 'And you, sir, what's your name?'

"Paragon of proper decorum, I smiled wanly at this bizarre woman. 'Robert O'Rourke.' I said. 'What a fabulous couple you make!' Ella squealed.

" 'Well, we're not actually...' I harumphed but Ella and her cameraman had already flitted off to the next table.

"One of the women turned to Camilla. 'Who on earth is that woman?'

" 'One of the Fitch cousins. Absolutely mad.'

"Had I known at the time what trouble this videotape was going to cause me, I would have hurried off after Ella Strand and smashed her camera."

"What trouble is that?" said Maurice.

"All in due time. Let me go on. I whiled away the evening, getting thoroughly soused, and discussing the finer points of breeding with my fellow horse owners. I attended the auction of paintings and sculpture, mostly equestrian oriented, and placed a couple of first bids on the reserve. Fortunately, I was immediately outbid and graciously retired from the fray. I tried to find Camilla Rouse to say goodnight but she had disappeared.

"The next morning when I rose feeling quite puffed up from my excursion into the land of the swells, I went down to the corner store to purchase a Racing Form and was startled to see the headline of the Springs Sentinel: JEWEL ROBBERY AT WYLIE GALA. I bought the paper and hurriedly read the lead to the article. It seemed that several hundred thousand dollars worth of precious gems had been stolen from the Wylie mansion during the charity auction. As yet the police had no clue as to the identity of the thief but it looked like 'an inside job.'

"You must understand, Maurice, how intrigued I was by this turn of events. So seldom is one present at an event of such consequence. After a waker-upper, I repaired to the track in order to bet the daily double in which my pal Vinnie Floppo had a mount. When the jockeys entered the saddling area. I called out to him with a friendly wave. Floppo looked at me askance.

" 'What are you doing here?' he asked. 'I am here to take in another day of equine entertainment and recoup yesterday's losses.'

" ' I'd get the hell out of here if I were you,' he said. 'Haven't you seen the TV?'

"In fact, I had not and had no way of knowing that Camilla Rouse and Harry Poon had skipped town and were the prime suspects in the jewel theft. That was hardly the worst of it. Ella Strand's videotape of the "fabulous couple" had been shown on the morning news and the police were eagerly looking forward to interviewing me. What to do?

"As a solid, upstanding citizen with little avenue of escape, I decided to brazen it out. I betook myself from the track, made my way across town, and strolled up the steps of the Springs rinky-dink police station where I presented myself to the desk sergeant.

" 'I am Robert O'Rourke,' I announced myself, 'and I understand that you wish to speak to me.'

"He looked at me as if he couldn't quite believe his eyes. 'Ah, yes,' he said. 'Could you just step over here?' He escorted me down the corridor to a door, which he politely opened, waved me in, and slammed it behind me. Maurice, I found myself in a jail cell."

"Not the first time."

"Of course not. But it certainly was the first time I could claim innocence of any crime. There was another individual in this cell, a doddering old fellow who looked up at me from the lower bunk with a crinkly smile and said: 'You know about Catherine the Great, don't you?'

" 'Well, not much,' I admitted. 'You will, you will.' He leaned towards me and looked around to make sure no one else was listening. 'She fucked horses,' he whispered. 'The way of the world,' I responded to this ancient bit of folklore. 'She fucked horses and the horses fuck us.' 'You don't understand,' he wheezed urgently. 'It was an assassination. Rasputin dropped the horse on her.'

"As little as I know about Russian history, I was fairly sure that Rasputin was not even born during the reign of Catherine the Great. 'Yes, of course,' I said. 'So you know!' he continued. 'And that's what started the Cold War.'

"There are worse things than being stuck in a jail cell with a babbling idiot but I can't think of one at the moment. He jabbered on and on until I was rescued by the desk sergeant who escorted me to a makeshift interrogation room where I was greeted by one Detective Barnes who bade me take a folding chair across a card table from him. 'Mr. O'Rourke,' he said, 'I understand you are a friend of Camilla Rouse.'

"I honestly replied,'.I barely know the woman.'

" 'That's not what we hear.'

" 'If you're talking about that videotape, it was simply an inopportune coincidence,' I replied. 'Wrong place, wrong time.'

" 'Who put your name on the Wylie guest list?'

" 'Miss Rouse. She thought I might be interested in purchasing a painting.'

" 'What made her think that?'

"I must say, Maurice, that Detective Barnes' line of questioning was beginning to make me distinctly uncomfortable. 'I have no idea,' I replied.

" 'But you did bid in the auction,' he pressed me. 'Just to be polite,' I said. 'I had no intention of buying anything.'

" 'So you're not only a charlatan and a con man but an auction shill as well.'

"Well, Maurice, I must say I was quite taken aback by this assessment."

"I'll bet you were. It's only one third wrong."

O'Rourke ignored this riposte and continued. " 'Are you impugning my good character?' I demanded with all the false dignity I could muster. 'I am a respectable citizen.'

" 'A respectable citizen who masquerades as a rich horse owner to attend society parties?' Barnes shot back. 'Excuse me, Detective, but I had an invitation.'

" 'From a woman who's wanted in connection with a robbery.'

"By now, I was sweating buckets, Maurice. This hick town flatfoot was trying to set me up as an accomplice to the crime. 'You've got me all wrong,' I protested. 'The first I knew anything about the robbery was when I read it in the newspaper this morning.'

" 'Where are you staying, Mr. O'Rourke?' he said. 'You wouldn't mind if we searched the place?'

"I had nothing to hide so I agreed to the humiliation of being driven in a police car to my temporary residence where passersby gawked like sideshow patrons as I was escorted into the building. The cops found nothing of interest and soon left me alone. I immediately decamped to the nearest saloon to ponder the meaning of this whole sordid affair."

"Meaning? What's to mean?"

"Everything that happens in life is connected, Maurice. The pattern may not be obvious, it may be almost invisible, but it is there. The chain of events that I brought upon myself by pretending to be someone I was not had caught up with me and given me a good spanking."

"Don't give me that shit," said Maurice. "You've spent your whole life pretending to be someone else."

"Precisely. And that's why I'm consigned to set some whiz kid, Wall Street asshole's backsplash this very day. Shall we proceed with the onerous job at hand?"

"Let's have another beer."

"Capital idea. Procrastination is the mother of harm reduction."

Maurice handed O'Rourke another can of St. Ives. "So what happened next?"

"The Springs."

"Oh yes. Against my better judgement I stayed on a few more days and was party through the press to the scandalous events that unfolded around the jewel theft. Camilla Rouse returned with a phalanx of lawyers and sued the Wylies for defamation of character. It seems that Mrs. Wylie was related to Camilla and that they'd never gotten along. Camilla not only claimed that the society doyen was making false accusations but that she herself had engineered the purported theft to claim the insurance money. She acidly pointed out that none of the many jewel theft cases in The Springs had ever been solved and insinuated that it was a sort of tradition for the rich lady 'victims' of these crimes to add to their pin money and defray their gambling losses during the racing meet by making spurious claims. Camilla found an immediate ally in the Wylies' insurer who refused to make payment until the situation was resolved. As you might imagine, all this caused quite a stir and Mrs. Wylie retaliated by calling Camilla a cheap tramp with a proclivity for unsavory gigolos and promising to prosecute her to the fullest extent of the law. However, no charges have yet been brought for lack of evidence.

"So you see, Maurice, the rich are different from you and I."

"How's that?"

"They are greedier."

With this parting observation, O'Rourke followed Maurice back through the window into the apartment and resumed the tedious labor which would certainly make neither of them rich. It was, after all, both their vocation and cruel destiny.

EPILOGUE

PH

The street where O'Rourke lives is not much different from any other street in the place where O'Rourke lives. The fall is funereal and the winter is brutally cold. In the spring, there are floods that leave two feet of mud on the street that dries as hard as concrete in the sun and has to be broken up with pickaxes and jackhammers. By August, there is always a water shortage and brown sediment runs from the tap.

At one end of the street where O'Rourke lives is a huge chemical plant that belches heavy brown smoke from its chimneys and fills the air with a sharp metallic tang. At the other end of the street is a nuclear power plant with a history of minor accidents and non-toxic leaks. Nearly everyone who lives on the street where O'Rourke lives has cancer. Or maybe it just seems that way. O'Rourke doesn't have cancer. At least, he doesn't think so.

Everyone who lives on the street where O'Rourke lives is worried about money. Nobody ever has enough of it. Everyone's fantasy is wealth and luxury and they spend hours dreamily discussing lottery tickets and imaginary fortunes in the bars and delicatessens and beauty shops on the street where O'Rourke lives. It makes them feel warm all over and they briefly glow with good feeling. What they want are big, flashy cars and fur coats and things like that. They do not want to live on the street where O'Rourke lives anymore but most of them will die there and they know it.

The people who live on the street where O'Rourke lives don't trust politicians or "big business" but they believe everything they read in the newspapers or see on television and can be whipped into a frenzy by almost any slight to their imagined "prestige". They are so gullible they can always be counted on to cut off their own noses in spite.

What they really crave is a war to relieve their boredom and sense of futility. The men think they would like to rape and pillage and bring massive death to some hated enemy. The women think they would like to be conquered and violated but emerge triumphant. Same old story. Their deepest cravings, however, lie in their own annihilation. Their despair is so huge and pervasive, the organism finds it almost insupportable; their instinct for self-preservation has been wiped out by their pain. That's the way things are with the people who live on the street where O'Rourke lives.

The apartment houses on the street where O'Rourke lives are mostly brick. The neighbors can see each other through their windows and hear practically anything that's going on in the immediate vicinity. On warm nights, O'Rourke used to sit at his own window and watch the couple who lived across the way, Tim and Tina, quarrel. One of their altercations he remembers particularly.

He was peering in their open window when Tina stormed into the room where Tim was sitting in his armchair reading the newspaper and pulsing with a low hum.

"I despise you!" she shrieked. "You nauseate me!" When she spoke, little yellow flakes congealed in the air and floated down on her husband like snow.

Tim's defenses began to disintegrate as Tina shot withering blasts from behind her dark glasses that left steaming holes in his field. Tim's head began to melt; his jowls surged over his shoulders and pulled his nose into a lava flow of flesh down his face. Abruptly, the steaming lake of molten head parted like the Red Sea and a cloud floated out through the crease. A band of bean shaped nodules moored the cloud to his head. In the cloud was a bone.

Tina was astonished. Little pointed, green plants began to grow from her scalp. "You're a fool, Tim," she hissed.

Tim began to radiate long waves with little hairs and Tina must have felt as if she was being assaulted by a colony of ants. An undulating green plant began to grow from the end of her nose and it didn't stop; soon it was twenty feet long, slimy and bright as okra. The plant coiled around Tim's leg and held him where he sat.

Tim was so humiliated, his head inflated and a balloon squeezed out of his mouth and hovered in the air between then like a small dirigible.

"So," he muttered bitterly.

The balloon floated slowly over Tina, rising and falling with the thermals, now almost grazing here head, then climbing high in the air. She gnashed her teeth and sharp bristles sprouted from the plant on the crown of her skull. It resembled a saguaro cactus and a miniscule peon nodded in the shade it cast across her head; at least until the balloon descended and exploded in a puncture flash of blue flame. Globs of burning jelly dripped from Tina's scalp and sizzled on the floor in a cloud of acrid fumes.

Tim coughed violently as the fingers of vapor

tickled the back of his throat and settled on his palette. The taste was oily and industrial. "So! That's it!" he wheezed in red-faced indignation. His nose burned with an incandescent glow and attracted swarms of flying insects. His head disappeared in a cloud of mosquitoes and gnats."

Tina was disturbed. "What are you cooking up in there?" she demanded.

Tim was delighted by the turn of events. He fired salvo after salvo of ion clusters from behind his insect screen; he barked like a dog. By this time, however, his nose was overheating. Patches of skin began to blister and curl like frying bacon and he was soon obliged to plunge his face into a basin of cool water where it hissed and sent up clouds of steam that dispersed the insect swarm.

Tim felt naked without his bugs and Tina pressed her sudden advantage. Her eyes welled with viscous, bitter tears that oozed slowly down the sides of her nose and crystallized on her upper lip. Inside the crystals were images that flickered in and out of focus, bleak little panoramas of vacant lots, rusty railroad tracks, abandoned piers.

The desolation hit Tim right in his gut. He doubled over and gasped as black fuzz closed in from the periphery of his vision and he felt himself receding from the world. His eyes went dull and white foam bubbled from his ears.

Tina brayed in triumph and did a little dance around her stricken husband. "My... old... flame..." she crooned.

Her victory celebration was somewhat premature however. Tim was reviving rapidly. The crown of his skull separated neatly from the lower part of his head and floated above his exposed brain. The brain turned bright orange and pulsed like a beating heart as the sharp odor of citronella filled the room and blue sparks shot from the inside of Tim's head.

Needless to say, Tina was taken aback by the devastating speed of her husband's recovery. The taste of conquest turned brackish in her mouth and she gagged convulsively as storm clouds rolled into the room through the open windows and obscured the ceiling. A kite with a brass key dangling from its tail blew out of Tim's open cranium and bobbed below the gusting clouds.

Tina covered her face with her hands and sobbed aloud. "You crummy bastard," she blubbered.

The air prickled with static just before a lightning bolt flashed and arced with the brass key. The charge rendered Tim translucent as an X-ray picture and he glowed greenish-blue as thunder cracked with gunshot snap! and rumbled across the room.

Driving rain poured from the clouds as Tina collapsed on the carpet and wailed: "I gave you the best years of my life! Now look at me! Just look at me!"

As suddenly as it had started, the storm was over. Tina lay sobbing on the floor in a puddle while Tim shook himself off. Soon her sobs turned into a low, growling drone that sounded like a distant outboard motor. Tim responded with a melancholy howl to set your hair on end.

Then the lights went out and O'Rourke couldn't see anything anymore. He could hear them, though, moving around in the dark. There was a crash that sounded like a lamp falling over simultaneous with the pop of an imploding light bulb.

O'Rourke heard Tina crooning, "Oh dogman... I will be your slave... my houndish darling..." and other similar endearments. Her voice had a faraway, trance-like quality that carried nothing of the intimate or even the affectionate. The room began to glow dull red and O'Rourke could hear Tina moaning rhythmically, building to a frightening lament and he knew that she would never be happy in this life.

Unfortunately, the light was not enough to illuminate anything. O'Rourke enjoyed watching other people in the heat of passion and occasionally attended the pornographic film theater on the street where he lives. Being that he took a special interest in Tim and Tina, he would have very much liked to study their sexual practices but never did he catch so much as a glimpse of their coupling.

Tim and Tina's quarrels were usually less spectacular than this one, but O'Rourke was seldom disappointed by their exhibitions. As time wore on, Tina seemed to gain more and more presence while Tim faded to translucence, transparence, and finally disappeared altogether. He was still there, though, because O'Rourke heard Tina nagging him from time to time.

Then the day came when Tina stopped talking to Tim. O'Rourke didn't know if he was there or not, but there was no evidence of his presence.

Sometimes he saw Tina sitting alone drinking elaborate cocktails that she mixed from a dozen different bottles on a little tea caddy. After she'd had a few, she often started laughing; ugly, harsh laughter with an uncontrolled hysterical edge. Other times she burst into tears and blubbered softly into her drink.

Her weight fluctuated wildly during this period. One day she might appear as shriveled and drawn as a concentration camp inmate, the next day her jowls and arms would quiver with excess flesh as she wheezed and puffed around the room.

She began to bring strange men back to her apartment. Some of them were brutish and vicious looking; most of them had no faces at all. After a few drinks the lights would go out and O'Rourke could hear Tina yowl like a cat as the men fucked her. He least he assumed that was what was going on because he couldn't see a thing, not even a dull red glow.

One day a moving van appeared on the street where O'Rourke lives and pulled up in front of the apartment house next door. Men in white overalls loaded the van quickly under Tina's nervous supervision. Then she got in a cab and followed the truck off down the street. O'Rourke never saw her again.

After Tina's abrupt departure, a retired couple moved into her former apartment. They sit in the living room where Tim and Tina used to quarrel and watch television. O'Rourke has never seen them do anything of any interest and consequently he doesn't look out the window much anymore.

Every now and again, O'Rourke goes to the corner tavern for a shot and a beer. Once, he thought he saw Tim sitting at the other end of the bar but it turned out to be a case of mistaken identity.